The Elitists

When the power brokers – the elite of Ravine River County – are in accord there is a good sense of law, order and justice. But when they fall out, as have the owners of a proposed new railroad with those of a steamboat company in the 1880s, the local community risks being destroyed.

The Elitists

K.S. Stanley

A Black Horse Western

ROBERT HALE

© K.S. Stanley 2019
First published in Great Britain 2019

ISBN 978-0-7198-3041-9

The Crowood Press
The Stable Block
Crowood Lane
Ramsbury
Marlborough
Wiltshire SN8 2HR

www.bhwesterns.com

Robert Hale is an imprint
of The Crowood Press

The right of K.S. Stanley to be identified as
author of this work has been asserted by him
in accordance with the Copyright, Designs and
Patents Act 1988

Typeset by
Derek Doyle & Associates, Shaw Heath
Printed and bound in Great Britain by
4Bind Ltd, Stevenage, SG1 2XT

PROLOGUE

With three sharp blasts on its whistle, the paddle steamer began to pull alongside the wooden quay, its stern wheel creating a wash down the river for as far as the eye could see. As she docked, her smoking funnels glinted in the warm, morning sunshine. Looking on from the quayside, her proud owner, Hilliard Rainecourt, removed his watch from his waistcoat pocket.

'Ten o'clock. She's done it,' Hilliard muttered to himself. 'She's bang on time.'

'Probity Quay, Probity Quay!' the captain shouted out. 'Twenty minutes stop!' The waterfront burst into life as passengers who had been waiting to board, appeared from the quayside bars and shops. The noise of their chatter blended with that of the people who were assembling on the bottom two decks of the Pride of Probity and preparing to disembark.

'Mornin', Mr Rainecourt, sir!' said the captain, addressing his employer from the bow of the boat.

'Good morning, Tom,' Hilliard replied. 'Does she handle well?'

'Like a dream, sir. She handles like a dream! The difference is so noticeable, especially at the bend, downstream where the river narrows.' Hilliard nodded. He understood

5

what the captain was talking about. Probity was perhaps a strange location in which to build a harbour and a small, some would say unusual, town on the clifftop above, for there were no connecting natural transportation routes in the vicinity. The width of the river, the low short bank on which the quay was built, and the steep hillsides at this point, however, provided adequate protection and space to moor the Rainecourt fleet on what was the main waterway of the region.

'I knew she would be good, Tom. I knew she would,' Hilliard Rainecourt replied enthusiastically. 'Anyway, I'll catch you later.' He touched the brim of his hat, acknowledging his respect for his captain and the man's opinion. Hilliard continued his walk along the quayside, greeting various people he knew as they also admired the latest addition to his fleet. The *Pride of Probity* wasn't quite the largest paddle steamer of the four that he owned but it was the fastest, the easiest to manoeuvre, and the most luxurious and expensive. Speed, flexibility, and comfort were all important to Hilliard but money wasn't. Not anymore.

Now in his early sixties, he had plenty of it. Three generations of Rainecourts had made their living from transporting freight and people on this stretch of river, each one continually improving and successfully expanding the business. Hilliard, however, wasn't in the super-rich league like the Vanderbilts. Unlike them, the Rainecourts had kept to the waterways and not diversified their investment into railroads. The Rainecourts had always respected the scientific evidence that 'it is easier to move an object on liquid than to carry it in a wheeled carriage' and therefore regarded the waterways as a far more sustainable source of income than the railroads. Although many people had made vast fortunes from them, far too many of the roads had been built speculatively, without a definite purpose, and it was clear to Hilliard that they were not the threat to inland water traffic that many people thought they would be. He foresaw many of the successful railroad entrepreneurs losing their fortunes and going bankrupt, ultimately because levels of demand would be too inconsistent to sustain the expenditure required to build new roads and maintain the existing ones.

That was not to say that Hilliard had never had setbacks in his life. Certainly, in the earlier days, he had experienced failure. In times of adversity, however, Hilliard's natural tenacity and resilience (and on occasion, use of some of his considerable fortune) had pulled him through such challenges in both his professional and personal life. For example, only a few years ago, he had lost his first young wife from tuberculosis, leaving him without a male heir to his business and estate.

The thought of being the last head of the Rainecourt dynasty had caused Hilliard much distress, so to rectify the situation he set his matrimonial sights on the young widow, Bella de Courcy, an intelligent and beautiful woman. Originally from the eastern seaboard, Ms de Courcy was some thirty years his junior. Hilliard soon found himself up against other suitors and realized that each in their own way was probably more eligible for the lady's hand than he might ever be. Undeterred, however, not only did he spend a sizeable 'war chest' from his personal fortune on jewellery and other precious gifts in order to win the fair lady's heart but he also made a great display of patience, politeness and humility, whenever he found himself in her presence.

Over time, the character failings of the other suitors, who were younger and less wise, revealed themselves and six months later, Isabella as she now preferred to be called, gave her hand in marriage to the most mature of her admirers, Hilliard Rainecourt. Having won for himself a lady who many regarded as a trophy wife, it seemed that all Hilliard needed to do now was await the good news of the arrival of a son, to whom he could pass on his legacy. He reasoned that a male heir to the throne of Hilliard Rainecourt was all that was needed, to make his life complete.

CHAPTER 1

'Quiet please, gentlemen!' the Chairman of the Transport Committee ordered firmly. 'We need to reach closure today regarding this application from the Ravine River Railroad Company to build a road over the hilltops, parallel to the Rainecourt Steamboat Company route.' There was an audible sigh from some members of the committee. The chairman looked at them disapprovingly, over the top of his glasses.

'This goes backwards and forwards, backwards and forwards,' said one of the committee, airing his frustration.

'I know, I know,' responded the chairman. 'But in the interests of being fair to all, there have been legitimate challenges and achieving resolution has resulted in delays and amendments. This application was always going to be contentious but it is time for the lobbyists on both sides of the argument to withdraw and remain silent, otherwise we in this room risk being accused of meddling in and distorting the process of government!' Normally a man to seek conciliation rather than confrontation, the chairman paused to catch his breath and adjust his glasses. 'Right!' he continued. 'Well, it is clear from the very fact that the railroad company has submitted such an application that they intend to compete with the steamboat company and we have to decide whether this is in the best interests of the local community and the state, in terms of both economic and social considerations. We have heard from and listened to various experts on this matter and the time has come to make a final decision. First, I will read out the key points made by the experts and then will ask if anyone has anything further to add but regardless, at five pm this afternoon we will vote on the matter and submit a recommendation accordingly. Is that OK?'

The committee members looked around the room at each other in silence and nodded their heads in approval. They had all had enough and knowing that the end of this particular journey was near, would be relieved to reach its destination, wherever that might happen to be. They had listened to their electorates, who been informed of the various pros and cons of the application by the newspapers. Some committee members had discreetly paid the proprietors of such journals to present their personal view as the newspapers' own, using money given to them by the waterways and railroad lobbies. A tainted democratic process perhaps, but one kept partially in check at least by the fact that the lobbies were not rich enough to buy everybody's opinion, especially that of the more insightful and vocally courageous.

'Good,' said the chairman. 'I will start with the waterways. Operationally, they have proven to be a success over a number of decades moving goods and people at an economic price, thus promoting prosperity and sustaining communities. In the past there has been a significant number of deaths through boiler fires and explosions on paddle steamers but better regulation and improved technology have greatly reduced these. Strategically, some see the transport infrastructure of the nation's future being largely based on the inland waterways. There are already hundreds of miles of navigable waterways, both north–south and east–west and these could be made deeper and the volume of silt reduced from upland erosion through greater use of forestation. Wider deployment of dams would ensure a constant flow of water all year round in areas where this currently is not the case. Proponents of these concepts believe these innovations, which are technically feasible, would enable bigger boats that ultimately would be able to carry more freight than a train. If this is the future, Ravine River County should be part of it.

'Now, let's turn to the railroads. The fact that they enabled the settlement of the interior and paved the way for innovations such as the telegraph cannot be denied. Indeed, they have transformed the nation. Operationally, with through lines it has been possible to transport goods hundreds of miles very quickly, opening up new markets and supply chains but sometimes closing others. There has been criticism from the anti-monopolists of discriminatory pricing whereby the roads have given different rates to different customers on the same routes. The rail companies argue that their policy of charging the maximum price that the freight can stand enables smaller customers to be subsidized rather than exploited and helps keep the trains loaded, making it cheaper for all. Everyone has heard a tale of abuse of such a policy but the anti-monopolist solution of more competition is leading to a strategic crisis with there being far too many railroads. Their customers may be enjoying a short-term bonanza of cheap rates but in the longer term this will not be sustainable and will lead to consolidation in the rail industry and a return to more realistic rates. The consequences of this process will inevitably be indiscriminate disruption to businesses and communities, potential failure even, which in a world, not driven by 'a race to the bottom' in terms of pricing, would not occur.

'So, gentlemen, if no one else has anything to say we will meet back here in an hour's time at five o'clock and take a vote on the matter!' The chairman was greeted by silence. The committee had been around this circular set of arguments too many times. 'By the way,' the chairman added as he got up to leave, 'there are seven of us so there will be no abstentions. We need a majority decision at five o' clock!'

'I have something to say,' said Senator Godefroy raising his hand, 'but I'll make it quick.' The chairman sat down again, as did everybody else. Godefroy with his usual impeccable sense of timing, took to his feet. Senator Godefroy had been a passive figure during the preceding debates, as was his way. He saw himself as the considered thinker and honest broker, although not all his colleagues would have described him in that way. Godefroy excelled at keeping his cards close to his chest, while all the time assimilating information. He said little but learned a lot. Not so much about the matter in hand; he was familiar with all the arguments but about his colleagues' behaviour. He observed and analysed their body language and the emotions in their voice, the way they used language and emphasised specific words. As a result, he thought he knew how each of them might vote on the current issue and deduced that he was probably the 'deciding' voter. However, he needed to make sure and try and win at least one other committee member over to his point of view.

'Well, Senator?' the chairman asked.

'First, I have to say I agree with the chairman's summary of what has been said on both sides of the argument. But I think we now need to apply this information more specifically to the application in front of us, which is effectively asking our permission for the Ravine River Railroad Company to compete with the Rainecourt Steamboat Company.

'The railroad indeed has been a disruptive innovation for the nation. It has changed markets, settlement patterns and indeed people's lives. Although people are very critical of railroad power, would they want all the track ripped up and things put back to as they were before? I very much doubt it. We are still learning to live with this phenomenon but we need to be careful when we start to interfere and tinker with the mechanisms of the market that ultimately determine prices, supply chains and most important of all, gentlemen, promote efficiency and effectiveness. The market does this automatically for us, of its own accord. If we were to carry out such a multi-faceted intervention, it would require surgical skill; not the cack-handed approach we frequently employ, where we seem to confuse passion and rhetoric with fact and analysis when debating the best way forward. This has led many to believe for example, that encouraging more competition will fix discriminatory pricing, only to find ultimately that blind pursuit of this particular cause and effect chain has brought us a surplus of railroads. A 'race to the bottom', as the chairman rightly points out, which is resulting in receiverships.

'I think we should accept this application and let the mechanisms of the market determine what should be, as much as possible. It seems less harm occurs when we don't interfere. It may be that there will be enough demand to support both rail and steamboat, although at the moment with the economy the way it is, that looks unlikely. So, what could happen, gentlemen? Well, either the railroad wins or the steamboat company does, that is the likelihood. There is another scenario: that in their battle to undercut each other, both companies go to the wall. If we were to see that start happening, which I believe is unlikely, then that would be the point for us to intervene. Not now, by turning the application down. Competition from the railroad could make the steamboat company more efficient and it would increase property values in the area. This is potentially a high-risk speculation on the part of the railroad company and I think, given all the problems the industry has been going through, we should trust they have done their sums correctly. I should also add that if you study the plans for the proposed route, you will find its construction has been so designed as to minimise damage to the surrounding countryside, particularly in terms of deforestation, thus avoiding unnecessary silting of the river. Thank you, gentlemen.'

There was a stir in the room as the committee members allowed the Senator's words to sink in. 'Thank you, Senator Godefroy,' the chairman said. 'Is there anybody else?' He looked sternly at his committee members. 'No? Good!' he exclaimed. 'See you all at five o' clock.'

CHAPTER 2

The door of the county jail opened at precisely 11am and allowed Carew Langdon to step out onto the street and into the hot June sunshine. He had finished his sentence, which had seemed like the longest eighteen months of his life and all for attempted armed robbery. He'd have felt better if it was for actual armed robbery but the charge sheet explicitly said 'attempted', which at least carried a lighter tariff. It wasn't much good for Carew's ego, however. Attempted was just a polite way of saying failed and he couldn't afford to have too many of those on his resumé. The next job needed to be a big one and a successful one.

He looked up and down the street. It was quiet with very few people about. There was no one to greet him, shake his hand, put an arm round him or tell him with a warm smile that they had missed him. But that was the way he wanted it. He was off to rendezvous with the others and needed to make sure that no one was following him. Each one of his gang was being released today, albeit from different prisons across the state. They were due to meet at sundown in the bar of a small, two-bit, run-down settlement, somewhere off the beaten track.

Carew walked across the street to the bank. He'd had many dreams about this place during the last eighteen

15

months. He'd often wondered if it was laid out inside how he had envisaged it through the bars of the meat wagon that had delivered him to the prison. He thought it was probably worth a peep inside. It could be a good proposition to put on the table later on for the boys to discuss, especially as this bank had some specific attractions. For example, under attack there was likely to be confusion amongst the staff. Should they try and raise the alarm and hope to get help from the prison wardens across the street? Or, at the sound of an alarm and any ensuing gunfire, would the wardens be more concerned about a potential riot in the prison and leave the bank staff to the mercy of the robbers? Also, the prison staff's wages were paid from the bank. It would be an embarrassing kick in the teeth for the justice system that it couldn't even protect and pay its own staff, their wages!

Cupping his hands on either side of his face, Carew peered through the window. The bank was smaller inside than he had expected but laid out much as he had reckoned.

'You got an account here, mister?' A guard, carrying a Winchester rifle against his shoulder, appeared from out of the shadows.

'No, but I was thinkin' about gettin' one. Would my money be safe in here?' The guard dropped the rifle to his waist and pointed the barrel at Carew.

'On yer way, cowboy an' don't even think about it!' He spat on the sidewalk and narrowed his eyes.

'No need to be like that, mister,' Carew said, smiling calmly. 'My investments could be big enough to pay for your next bonus, which no doubt you think you deserve but now, thanks to your surly attitude, I'll guess we'll never know.' He turned on his heel and walked down the street to the livery stable. Having agreed on a price for a horse, he saddled up and, much to the consternation of the bank guard, circuited

the street twice to satisfy himself that he was not being followed, before going on his way.

Carew arrived at the bar mid-afternoon, a few hours before
the others. He ordered a bottle of whiskey and sat down in a
shaded corner. The alcohol tasted as good as the freedom he
now enjoyed. Apart from the occasional fly, seeking refuge
from the heat outside, and the barman, who spent more time
sat out the back than behind the bar, the place was empty
and Carew was able to focus his mind on how the gang might
rob the bank opposite the prison. Deep in thought, he was
initially unaware of the two strangers who had arrived and
had sat themselves down in the opposite corner. As he took a
brief break from his mental machinations to pour another
glass of whiskey, he became aware of their presence. They
looked of no consequence, just two more drifters on the trail,
but as he started to eavesdrop their conversation Carew
became more and more interested.

'The tracks have still got rust on 'em though, ain't they,
Judd? I thought the line was abandoned.'

'Well it certainly was, Marvin, certainly was. But talk is that
they've reopened the mine five miles north of here.
Someone's found a new vein close to the old shaft. Only been
opened a week, an' they're runnin' a special one-car train
tomorrow at midday, to the mine. Rumour is that it contains
a stack of cash, for the workers' wages, purchasin' supplies
and so on. Liquidity, you know to get the place started again.
No bank up there, not as yet anyhow.'

'But there ain't that many workers up there surely to
warrant a wages train for their pay. Stagecoach maybe but not
a train.'

'You might think that, Judd but apparently there's nearly
a hundred of 'em. They've started openin' up the bars and
dance halls again. They're expectin' another gold rush.'

'So, how'd you find that out, Marvin?'

'Well, I was ridin' up the valley the other day and there were men from the railroad company repairin' the track. Got talkin' to one of 'em. He told me about it. Reckons there's far more gold in them hills than they ever thought there was before.'

'Mmm,' said Judd. 'Be good for the folk who live around these parts, then.'

'Sure will,' Marvin replied. 'That's why old Mac here hasn't tried to sell this damned bar. If it all takes off he could stand to make a fortune. Ain't you noticed he's started smilin' again of late?'

'Yep. I have. Wondered why that was. Hey, it's time to go, Marv. The sun's movin' round off the verandah, look. You ready?'

'Yes,' said Marvin, draining his glass. 'Let's go.'

That's very interesting, Carew thought to himself. I've not only got my first proposition but those two drifters have given me another idea that I can put to the boys as well.

'Listen, as the owner of this company, I tell you we have no alternative!' Burrell Challener slammed the palm of his hand down on the boardroom table. 'Thanks to Senator Godefroy's rousing speech at the committee meeting the state legislature has awarded us the charter so that we can compete with Rainecourt's steamboats. It is our lifeline. C'mon, what's the matter with you?'

'Well,' said the chief finance officer. 'To start with, where will we get the funds from to build the road? Won't be cheap, either, crossin' the tops of those steep hills. I can't afford to put any more of my personal money into the business.'

'We'll borrow it like we normally do. Issue some more bonds,' Burrell retorted.

'But we can't afford to pay the dividends on the last set, at least not out of operating profits. By virtue of what we do, we carry high fixed costs that are incurred regardless of customer revenues. You know that. If they're not met, we'll face the receiver.'

'You're the accountant, cook the books. Normal rules apply: pay the dividends out of the income from the sale of the new bonds but boost new construction in the books by the same amount, so that it appears that the income from new bond sales is all being spent for its intended purpose of building more road. We'll finance the shortfall by spending less than the books say we have on repairs and maintenance. It's called robbin' Peter to pay Paul.'

'It's more like robbin' Peter to pay Peter!' the chief finance officer snapped back.

'Look it's not my fault,' Burrell Challener quickly pointed out. 'I didn't want to run the business like this. I am being forced by other people to behave like this! People wanted railroads but when the bills dropped on their doorsteps they didn't wanna pay the full costs of them. We can't afford to run freight cars half empty. If someone comes to us and they genuinely can't pay the goin' rate, we ain't gonna turn 'em away. Some income is better than none. On the other hand, if a regular customer is considerin' using another line or steamboat, then of course, we're gonna give 'em a discount.

'But people see that as monopolistic price fixing and as a result want more competition. So, afraid of increased regulation and worse, we oblige and build more roads, wherever we think there are routes from which we can extract sufficient business. We keep the whole merry-go-round spinning, but only by ruthlessly competing with other railroads and the waterways. A conventional business, faced with more competition, would reduce its costs but we can't do that easily because we need to keep our infrastructure running. Operators are gonna go to the wall, an' it's all because of the people, who just don't get it!'

'Perhaps we should do more to inform them,' the chief finance officer suggested.

'We have!' Burrell slapped the palm of his hand down on the boardroom table again. 'We've spent shedloads of money with newspaper editors in the towns along our routes to persuade them to write articles explaining how we are obliged to operate and what a good job we're doin'. They promote us well cos they know I'll cut 'em off if they don't!'

'Folk are sayin' we take too much money out of this business for our own private use,' the chief operating officer commented. 'They see us as being extremely wealthy and all at the expense of the fare paying customer.'

'An' that goes to prove my point, that folk just don't get it!' Burrell exclaimed. 'The three of us have got rich not from transporting passengers and freight, as people might think, but from the increase in land values, and property development that building railroads has enabled along its routes. I keep sayin' to you boys, we are really a land speculation company, not one whose sole purpose is to run railroads. We are speculators, not transport chiefs.

'Speculatin' in land, as in anythin' else, whether it's gold mining, silver mining or whatever, is a high-risk business, which means that when it's successful it offers very high reward.'

'So, if really we are land speculators, how's it gonna help us financially to compete with the Rainecourts? There is not enough traffic along that river or ever likely to be to support two businesses,' the chief operating officer pointed out.

'I think that's the railroad man in you talking,' Burrell suggested. 'The speculator in you should think like this. The key differentiator for the railroad is speed. We are much faster than the steamboats. People will like that, especially when we undercut the steamboat rates to tempt them to try us. We'll take Rainecourt's business so we can buy his steam-boat company at a rock-bottom price, although it will be in a different name from this company so that it doesn't look like a monopoly. Then, we'll ship the high-value light goods such as coffee and wine by rail and continue to ship the heavy raw materials such as coal by steamboat!'

'So effectively, customer requests to transport goods are received and collated by a "holding company", which will "invite" the rail and steamship companies to bid for the transportation as appropriate?' the chief operating officer intervened.

'Exactly!' Burrell agreed. 'That is the goal from a trans-port perspective, which by itself won't make us or anyone else rich. From a speculator's perspective, however, the big prize is that beautiful small town of Probity. Property values are already high there but with a railroad on the doorstep and Rainecourt out of the way, the value of the buildings, the land that they're standing on and the surrounding hinter-land will go through the roof!' He paused to allow his fellow directors to take it all in.

'But we've looked at building a line to and beyond Probity before and the upfront cost of building through those hills was prohibitive,' the chief finance officer challenged.

'Be much cheaper this time,' Burrell assured him. 'I'd already hired on a retainer while we were awaiting the deci-sion from the charter committee a man who's a top engineer and a brilliant mathematician. What he doesn't know about grades, curvature and cost efficiency just ain't worth knowin'.'

'This has the potential to get ugly,' the chief operating officer pointed out. 'Rainecourt's never gonna give up every-thing he's worked for without a fight. Our workers could be exposed in those hills. It could get really nasty.'

'Don't worry about that either,' Burrell replied. 'I've thought about that as well. The matter is in hand.'

*

Carew indicated to each of his four gang members to crouch down in the undergrowth by the side of the rusty track. There were three of them on one side, with Carew and his deputy, Smokey, on the other and five minutes to go until midday. He was nervous. The gang had gone for this alternative as opposed to robbing the bank. Holding up a wages train, in a secluded area in the middle of nowhere, was a total no-brainer for them compared with robbing a bank opposite a heavily guarded prison. Carew hadn't told them how he'd heard about this opportunity. In retrospect it sounded a little too good to be true. But he knew from the way that he had told them that they were very impressed and glad to have him running the show once more. He didn't let them see it but those remaining minutes leading up to midday were anxious ones for Carew: what if the train didn't arrive?

With a minute to spare, however, and much to his relief, he could hear in the distance the rhythmic sound of a steam train. Full of confidence, he sprang into action. He removed the cheroot from his mouth and held the lighted end against a piece of broken branch. As the dry wood started to smoke and catch alight, he placed the branch in the bottom of the ten-foot -high bonfire they had built across the track. It was a ploy he had heard his uncles talk about from their Civil War days, when they wanted to stop ammunition trains.

As the train came around the bend and the crew saw the fiery obstacle in front of them, they applied the brakes and the engine, tender and caboose slid to a halt just yards away from the fire. 'Get down now all of you or we'll torch the train!' Langdon shouted, brandishing his gun. The four-man crew alighted from the train with their hands in the air. 'Take any weapons they have and watch over 'em,' he ordered his gang. 'Smokey,' he called out. 'You come with me. Think there might be a safe on board for you to blow open!'

The two men entered the caboose from its rear platform. Smokey looked surprised. Having robbed trains before, he was expecting the caboose to have been turned into a small, personalised lounge for the conductor's personal comfort. 'There's, there's nothin' here,' he stammered. 'There's no safe, nothin'!'

'What about that cupboard over there?' Carew said, feeling a sharp dose of adrenalin coursing through his body. Smokey did as he was bid.

'Just this leather satchel,' Smokey replied. He took out a knife from his boot and levered the locked clasp open. 'Here we are!' he exclaimed. 'This looks like what we're lookin' for. All neatly enveloped!'

'Let me see!' Carew demanded, full of excitement. He crossed the caboose in one stride, grabbed the satchel from Smokey's arms and emptied the contents on the floor. Down on his knees, he tore open an envelope and took out the pile of notes. 'They're not printed on!' he said angrily. He tore open the next envelope only to find more blank pieces of paper. 'We've been set up!' he cried out as he grabbed his gun.

'All of you outside now, hands in the air, guns on the ground!' a voice boomed out across the narrow valley. 'You're completely surrounded!' Carew peered through the caboose window. He could see at least ten men, who had been lying low on the hillside. They had their rifle sights firmly fixed on the caboose and the people by the side of the train. Carew thought briefly about whether they should risk a shootout. The odds were not good. Not only were his men surrounded but they were outnumbered as well. He threw his gun over the hand rail of the caboose's rear platform and ordered Smokey to do the same. With their hands in the air, they walked off the train.

A man dressed in a smart suit with a patterned waistcoat and a pocket watch came to greet them at the bottom of the steps. 'Carew Langdon?'

'Yes, mister,' the outlaw replied.

'Used to ride with my kid brother, Hiram Challener, in the early days, didn't yer? Expect you heard he got caught and was hung.'

'Yep, that's right, mister. I'd heard about that. Hiram taught me a lot of what I know.'

'Hmm, well one thing you do seem to have learnt from him is that bravado rarely makes up for bad planning. Hiram would have tried to shoot his way out of this situation, which is why he is no longer with us, but you have chosen not to, which is smart. So, listen carefully, Langdon cos here's the deal. I am Burrell Challener, the railroad entrepreneur, and you have just attacked one of my trains, threatened my men and tried to steal the cash on board. For that, I could have you an' your boys sent back to prison for attempted armed robbery. Again.'

'It wouldn't hold up in court, Challener,' Langdon replied. 'There wasn't any cash on board.'

'Oh yes there was,' Burrell replied, you just didn't look in the right place, Carew. Perhaps you ain't so smart.' Carew Langdon looked puzzled.

'I set you up, Langdon. Those two men you overheard talking in the bar yesterday afternoon?' Carew nodded. 'Well, they work for me. I had them follow you from the prison yesterday. Good, aren't they? You never suspected a thing. But that's the standard I expect from my workers. So, where were we? Prison, yes. On one hand I could have you sent back there?'

'And on the other?' Carew asked, very much hoping for a better offer.

'On the other hand, you and your boys could work for me.

24

Good pay, steady work. Prefer that?'

'It sounds better so far but what would we be doin'?'

'You would be my rail company's special security team. Not checkin' whether folk have paid their fares or stuff like that but defending us from and attacking our enemies, as and when I say so. Strong-arm stuff basically. Interested?' Burrell Challener asked, offering Carew Langdon his hand. Langdon looked at his men for signs of affirmation.

'Yes, Mr Challener,' Langdon replied, shaking Burrell's hand. 'Me and the boys are.'

'Now, you may have been wondering, Langdon, why I have gone to all this trouble to offer you a job. You see, in many ways you an' I are similar. We both attempt to make a living from using other people's money. The difference in operation is that I borrow it, invest it and then pay people back, whereas you steal it and then spend it. I am very successful and generally operate legally, though I may push the boundaries on occasion, whereas you are not successful and operate illegally. Now, the interesting thing about the work I want you to do is that you'll almost inevitably end up having to operate on both sides of the law. Which is where I think we will make a good team. You will take your orders from me. If you disobey them or are disloyal and try to undermine or betray me, you'll all be back in prison, quick as a flash. Understood?' Carew Langdon nodded. 'So, do we have a deal?'

'Yes, Mr Challener. We do,' Langdon replied.

'Good. You and your boys are all on the payroll, as of now.'

CHAPTER 3

For someone still only in his late twenties, the youthful-looking gentleman had already enjoyed a life rich in experiences, but spending the night on a paddle steamer had not been one of them. When he boarded the *Pride of Probity* on that June afternoon, however, he was more than surprised at the standard of comfort. He had decided to rent a state room for two or three nights, which compared with many hotel rooms he had stayed in, was far superior with its luxurious wall fabrics and stylish furnishings. On the other hand, it wasn't cheap but as a base to get to know the place, it was near the action and he felt he deserved a treat. Besides, the card tables in the grand saloon enjoyed a good reputation and his key recreational pleasure was playing cards for money.

Other than for business purposes, he was not a man overly interested in socializing, so he took a light evening meal alone in his state room. His other recreational pleasure was drinking fine wine and enjoyable as that would have been on this occasion, he refrained as he planned to play cards and did not want any of his faculties to be impaired. At eight o' clock precisely, he left his suite and made his way to the grand saloon. As he walked along the deck he noticed how much the outside temperature had dropped. Although it had been a fine day, it had turned into one of those occasional cold summer evenings when access to a warm fire was welcome.

In the warmth of the grand saloon, he went to the bar and ordered himself a glass of chilled water with a slice of lemon and proceeded to sip it slowly while he studied the card players. His main focus soon arrested on a man, probably in his early forties, playing at the table in the corner. The quality of the man's suit, with its ill-fitting, baggy sleeves, implied that he wasn't wealthy but the young gentleman thought that the man would make sure his demeanour suggested otherwise. He noted the man's attempts to occasionally engage his opponent in light conversation, which he surmised was probably of a convivial but superficial nature.

The young gentleman had often observed this type of behaviour in poorly dressed card players, which in his experience normally indicated a high degree of self-interest, coupled with low levels of integrity and intellect. He decided to change his position at the bar and rest on his other elbow, so as not to attract attention that the man in the corner had become a specific focus of interest for him. After five minutes, he moved his position back again, only to find that the man's opponent had changed and the man appeared to have significantly increased his winnings, judging from the amount of cash now on the table and the smile on his face. The pattern repeated itself twice over the next half hour or so with two more opponents quitting after losing what looked like considerable sums of money.

It all suggested to the young gentleman that the convivial but superficial character sat in the corner was probably cheating. Successful card players invariably dress well, not least because they can afford to. This character's dress suggested that he did not appear to win on a regular basis and, if indeed he indulged in bland and trivial conversation, that would also suggest he probably did not possess the intellectual sharpness to be a successful player. Yet tonight he was winning continuously against players who could afford to lose considerable sums of money.

The one type of card player that the young gentlemen hated with a vengeance was the cheat. For him, they totally destroyed the dignity and science of the activity and should never be allowed near the tables to fleece other people of their money. He moved along the bar to where the last loser was having a consolation drink. 'Good is he, that man you just played?'

'I wouldn't say that,' the loser said. 'To be frank, I'm shocked. I play here regularly and to a good standard as well and I am sure I had each game covered. But he beat me every time. I don't know how he did it.' Acknowledging the man's disappointment, the young gentleman patted him on the shoulder before walking over to the corner table, where the victim's seat was empty again.

'Mind if I have a game with you,' he asked the poorly dressed man, who was busy counting his winnings.

'No sure, be my guest,' the man said. 'Be glad to pass the time with you. I can play for another half hour or so. I am staying in Probity itself tonight on the top of the cliff. Have you been up there?' Without waiting for an answer, he continued talking. 'It's very exclusive, you know. I have friends there and a small bit of business to attend to in the morning.'

'I've heard a bit about it,' the young gentleman replied. 'But I haven't been there.'

'No, well, not everyone can afford it up there, you know. You need money to use the facilities there, let alone live there. Most folk couldn't afford to stable a horse for a night, in Probity. I've travelled here by river. Do you know what time the stagecoach takes people from down here to the cliff top?'

'I believe it goes on the hour and every half hour with the

last one leaving here at midnight,' the young gentleman replied. He paused momentarily. 'Yes, that's right,' he continued thoughtfully. 'It's the last one coming back down that is at ten past midnight. Anyway, my good man. At what game would you care to play me?'

The young gentleman felt relaxed but he sensed his opponent becoming jittery as his pile of winnings gradually reduced. 'I thought you could only play for half hour or so?' the young gentleman enquired. 'It's nearly half past ten now and we've been playing for well over an hour.'

'I know. But you have taken a lot of my winnings from me. You are very good.'

'I'm one of the best,' the young gentleman replied in a matter of fact way.

'Look, I'll tell you what I'll do. At my peak this evening, I must have had twice as much as I have now. I'll stake the rest on one last game.'

'OK, fair enough,' said the young gentleman. 'I'll match your amount.' He added his share to the stake money while his opponent, shuffled the cards. The young gentleman cut the pack and then his opponent dealt the hands.

The young gentleman knew that if his opponent was going to cheat it would happen imminently in this last game. His mental powers and his ability to count the cards were most important at this point. He felt some sort of presence suddenly pass behind him. It was strange; as if someone had looked over his shoulder and read his hand as they walked past. Either that, or someone with a powerful aura had entered the room. Instinctively, he looked behind him. It was the latter. A statuesque woman in a powder blue dress complete with a bustle and silk and satin skirt overlays glided majestically across the saloon to the bar, radiating her presence as she went. She paused and spoke briefly to the head bar tender. Her open countenance suggested that she was someone who, although very confident and self-assured, was not given to arrogance. She gave the bar tender a warm smile and then left the room. She was the most beautiful woman the young gentleman had ever set eyes on.

'That's Mrs Rainecourt,' his opponent informed him. 'Her husband owns everything in this place.' He laid a winning hand down on the table. The young gentleman looked stunned.

'The ace of spades there,' he said, pointing at the card in the winning hand. 'It's already gone. I counted it earlier.'

'I'm afraid you must have been mistaken,' the young gentleman's opponent said as he started to gather up his winnings. 'I think the presence of Mrs Rainecourt temporarily distracted you and your counting. Don't worry. She has that effect on lots of men.'

'No! You pulled the ace when I wasn't looking. You probably concealed it in your baggy sleeve, waiting for the opportunity to play it. Like I told you, I'm one of the best and not only can I count the cards but I can remember the order in which each card was played. Let's check, shall we?' In his anger, the young gentleman stood up too hastily and accidently knocked the table. His opponent put his arm out quickly to avoid his drink falling over and in doing so knocked the pile of discarded playing cards to the floor. He bent down, gathered up the fallen cards and as he stood up mixed the ones still on the table back into the pack.

'Sorry,' he said. 'I'll guess you'll never know for certain as to whether the ace got played twice or not but I swear to you that I am no cheat. I have beaten you fair and square, which I guess means that, in your words, I can also say that I'm one of the best. Goodnight!'

*

Very excited by his winnings, and the prospect of a night in the luxurious Probity Grand Hotel paid for 'out of his own money', the man in the ill-fitting suit knew he would have to lose himself and disappear into the crowd. He'd turned over several punters in the last few hours and he didn't want any of them on his back, spoiling the rest of his evening. He was proud at how well he'd played it, especially with the arrogant, patronizing young gentleman, who was so full of intellectual airs and graces. Proud, not just with the way he had played the cards but that he had let his smug opponent know that he was a man of means as well, with connections in Probity. The young gentleman did know that he was intending to be on one of the last three stagecoaches but he hadn't mentioned specifically which one. The others he had fleeced knew nothing about his intended movements.

It was a gamble as to which stagecoach he should take up the cliff to Probity but he decided on the middle one, half an hour before midnight. To rush off the boat and catch the eleven o' clock might be too obvious. He wondered if he may have been too arrogant; boasting about being able to afford to mix with the Probity set. He decided, however, to put these pessimistic thoughts behind him. It was time to indulge in a brief celebration: a moment to savour and enjoy some of his considerable winnings. An amount that in total even his smart-arsed brother would be impressed by. Then there was all the other news he had to pass on as well; shame his brother wasn't here. OK, so he hadn't won the money fairly but cheating at cards and getting away with it, especially against regular gamblers, required a significant amount of skill and effort.

There was time to spare before the 11.30 stagecoach left the quay for Probity, so he decided to have a couple of stiff drinks and lose himself in the crowd. There was a limited choice of places to visit but he chose a rough bar at the far end of the quayside: a place where his type of people could enjoy themselves and where any possible pursuer would feel very uncomfortable about creating a scene.

At just after twenty-five minutes past eleven o' clock, the now slightly tipsy card cheat boarded the stagecoach for the short ride to Probity town on top of the cliff. He was surprised to find sat opposite him a man – a stranger in fact – who barely acknowledged him. The man seemed to be well wrapped up against the cold summer night with a long overcoat, a Stetson and a scarf that covered his mouth and nose. Satisfied that this wasn't the angry young gentleman he had conned earlier, the card cheat sat back in his seat for the five-minute ride to the Probity Grand Hotel.

The ride up the cliff face was basically a zig-zag: a series of steep climbs, each punctuated at its end by a tight, one hundred and eighty degree turn into the next climb. On the second ascent the stranger leant forward and hit the card cheat with a blow on the head from the butt of a revolver. As the coach turned into the next hairpin bend, the stranger rummaged through the cheat's satchel but, unable to find any cash, started to strangle the cheat with the bag's strap. When the stage approached the end of the third ascent, the cheat was semi-conscious. The driver slowed down ready to take the next one hundred and eighty-degree bend and as he did so the riverside door opened and the card cheat fell out of the coach, losing his jacket in the process. The gush of cold air as he fell down the cliff face temporarily started to revive him but it was bouncing off the rocks into the river below that finally killed him.

As the coach slowed down to turn into the fourth hairpin, with the driver noisily struggling to control the horses, the stranger slipped out of the cliff-side door, checked what had happened to his fellow passenger and then proceeded to bury his own coat and scarf in between the rocks. He climbed the final twenty yards of his journey on foot, reaching the top just after the stage arrived at its destination.

'Well, I'll be damned,' said the driver to the ticket seller. 'Who would believe it? I had two passengers on board at the start and both of them vanished into thin air. I never saw or heard the leaving of them either!'

'Probably slipped out on one of the bends for a piss and are now walking the rest of the way,' the ticket seller said. 'Half of 'em ain't as fancy as they think they are. Wanna ticket down to the quayside, mister? Last trip tonight.'

'Yes please,' said the stranger, adjusting the brim of his hat low over his eyes.

CHAPTER 4

Isabella Rainecourt sat on the window seat in her drawing room, which looked out onto the town square and across the river below. It was a magnificent view that would have lifted the spirits of even the saddest person. She would often sit there and sew but today she chose just to sit and reflect, while allowing herself to be refreshed by the beauty of nature; an inspirational gift, free for all humanity to enjoy. She was saddened that so many often seemed oblivious to its presence.

The town of Probity was also a gift, or at least the money for it was, given to Isabella by her husband, Hilliard, as a more than generous wedding present. The design of the town had been Isabella's brainchild and she had set to work on its detail as soon as they decided to marry. Hilliard saw the town as their joint contribution to the Rainecourt legacy. Isabella had based its design on the typical European medieval town, with its central square surrounded by buildings and a small garden area in the middle adorned by trees and public benches. In one of the corners adjacent to the Rainecourt mansion, she had a church built, similar to those found in English villages. At the far end of the square, facing the roadway that descended the cliff face through a series of hairpin bends to the river and Probity Quay, stood the Probity Grand Hotel. The Grand, as it was known locally, also owned additional rooms in a similar building, which again faced the road but from the opposite corner. Like the Grand, the other buildings around the square were similar in style to those found in successful western towns that once stood on the frontier. There was an opera house and theatre, a dance hall, a provisions' store, coach makers, livery stables and so on.

Isabella had chosen this design because she wanted Probity to have and be known for two main characteristics. First, she wanted a town that had the aesthetic layout of a traditional European town but which exuded the tranquil air of an English village; a place where people who upheld the Victorian cultural values of a successful western town could feel very much at home. The second characteristic, which was at least as important to her as the first, was exclusivity. People who wanted to live in Probity certainly needed to have money to be able to afford to buy property. That kept many of the colourful characters, who were always on the make and frequented the gambling hall and the quayside bars and whorehouses, with their kind, down by the river. But not necessarily all. Even rogues got rich but they would inevitably fail the next test: censure by the Probity Property Committee, who bought and sold all the property in the town. All powerful, they ended up deciding who could live in Probity. Their judgements, however, could be flexible in exceptional circumstances. For example, the town's preacher, a man of high virtue but few assets, was allowed to rent his accommodation at very favourable rates. That did not mean to say that others, also of high virtue but with little means, were totally excluded. Depending on their circumstances, they could be awarded benefits from the Probity Benevolence Fund, a not ungenerous charity run by Isabella and her small band of ladies who discreetly governed the social and cultural activity of the town.

*

There was a knock on the drawing room door. 'Come in,' Isabella called out.

'I am sorry to disturb you, Mrs Rainecourt.' It was the maid.

'That's alright, Eleanor,' Isabella replied. 'What is it?'

'A young gentleman called at the front door. He wanted me to give you this.' She passed her employer a sealed envelope. 'He asked to meet with you and wanted to stay but I explained that it was neither convenient nor appropriate but if he left his name, and you wanted to see him, you would get in touch with him.'

'And did he?' Isabella asked, slightly bemused by the young gentleman's effrontery.

'Yes, he said his name was Isham Griffen, ma'am.'

'Fine. Thank you, Eleanor. That's all for now.' After the maid had shut the door, she sat down again on the window seat and opened the envelope, which was addressed to herself. She took out the letter inside and read its brief content. She felt her heart race. Could those few words be true or was it some form of a joke? She read them again. She took a few deep breaths. She knew she would need to take some form of action. She picked up the bell from the small round table by her seat and rang for her maid.

'Eleanor,' she said as the servant entered the room. 'I need you to get in touch with this Isham Griffen. If he is available, I will see him here, at four o'clock tomorrow afternoon.'

'Yes, at once. Thank you, ma'am,' the maid said. Isabella waited until Eleanor had closed the door and swore under her breath. Could this be connected with her past history in some way? Surely not? If that had been coming back to haunt her, the ghosts of her past would have surely made their presence

36

felt a long time ago. Wouldn't they? Isabella started to cast her memory back.

The transformation of Isa Courcy, as her parents called her when she was a small girl on the eastern seaboard, to Izzy Couer – the variation on her name she adopted when she arrived in the cattle towns in her late teens, to plain Belle – the outlaw's woman – and finally to Isabella de Courcy – the mature woman who had reclaimed her birthright, was so well crafted that everyone believed that she had always been a widowed aristocrat from the Atlantic coast, who having decided to seek a new life elsewhere, had headed west. People who questioned her about her past life were given short shrift.

'I'm afraid it is my past,' she used to tell them politely. 'Not yours. You were never part of it. If, however there are bits of it which may be relevant to us both enjoying a better future, I will gladly share those with you.' Not even her husband challenged her regarding her back story. He had his own vision of his wife and he didn't want that fantasy tainted by a different reality. There was only one person still in her life who was part of her past and knew the truth and that was Bose Hendry, the sheriff of the particular cattle town she had lived in, who ended up becoming Isabella's confidant and father figure.

Isabella's parents had sent her to live with her aunt in one of the cattle towns of the Midwest when she was in her late teens, to experience the wider world, in the belief that such a lifestyle would only serve to reinforce the Victorian moral values of her upbringing. The naive but curious Izzy initially found it a strange world, especially in the summer months when the cowboys came to town, drinking, fighting, gambling, and womanizing. They didn't give a hoot about Victorian values, which appeared to have no bearing whatsoever on their lives, yet at the same time the townsfolk carried on their own way of life, tolerating this seasonal, feral, human invasion, albeit under sufferance. Neither side seemed to benefit philosophically nor spiritually from the presence of the other, and Izzy soon worked out that the only tie that kept them together was money. If the townsfolk could temporarily suspend their pride and feeling of superiority derived from the belief that they owned the moral high ground and provide their itinerant summer population with alcohol, loose women, gambling and exclusive premises in which to enjoy those pastimes, then they would become wealthy. The hypocrisy of this situation however, didn't reinforce Izzy's belief in the values of her upbringing – it almost destroyed them.

By the time she was in her early twenties, Belle, as she was now known, had long left her aunt's home and was living with a young man called Hiram Challener, who had a reputation for being a bit of a gunslinger. The one thing they had in common was that they had both become the black sheep of their respective families. 'One day, I'm gonna be rich like my brother, Burrell,' he used to tell Belle. 'He's buildin' a railroad to this town, yer know. Put the place on the map, if I don't put it there before him,' Hiram told her with a twinkle in his eye. They lived well enough on Hiram's wages as a stock man, occasionally topped up by his winnings at the tables. That was until the day that Hiram, as he had promised, decided to put the town on the map.

Unbeknown to Belle, robbing the town bank was the big plan to make the town famous and make Hiram as rich as his brother. To be good at anything there is nothing quite like serving an apprentice under a very competent master, but neither Hiram nor his crew had had this experience. As a result, the staff stood their ground, the gang panicked and Hiram shot the head bank clerk. By the time they had arrived penniless at their hideaway a few miles out of town, the bank clerk had died and the gang was being hunted for armed robbery, with Hiram personally wanted for murder.

It was Sheriff Bose Hendry who sought out Belle to try and learn of the Challener gang's whereabouts. He begged her to tell him where Hiram was hiding. The sheriff pointed out that harbouring a murderer was a very serious offence and claiming that she didn't know of Hiram's whereabouts would not be a sufficient defence, especially if subsequently it turned out that she knew all along. It was a moment of deep crisis for Belle, bringing the contradiction between her new values and Izzy's old ones into painfully sharp focus. But Bose didn't push her. He empathized with her position, and calmly talked it through with her. Then came her epiphany, the moment in which Belle became Isabella, the realization that her old values transcended the gluttonous, gratuitous ones of Belle's lifestyle and underpinned the dignity of the meaning of life.

Having surrendered the details of her lover's hideout to the law and while his deputies rode out there to make the arrest, Bose arranged for the fast departure of Isabella to a safe place across the state line. It was there that he helped her to build a new identity: that of society lady Isabella de Courcy. He supported and encouraged her to work her way up to this new role via a fictitious, transition stage where she publicly presented herself as the recently widowed Bella de Courcy.

Thus it was that Bose and Isabella came to make a pact between them: that the story of her life in the cattle town would be their secret and as long as it stayed that way this part of her past would not catch up with her. If, for whatever reason, it did and harm was threatened then she was to get in touch with Bose straight away.

As Isabella got up from the window seat to busy herself in order to calm her mind, she wondered if that moment might be close to hand.

CHAPTER 5

'Ma'am,' Eleanor said. 'Your visitor is here.'

'Thank you, Eleanor,' Isabella replied. She walked towards the door, where a handsome man stood in the doorway. She presumed him to be of a similar age to herself.

'Isham Griffen, ma'am. Pleased to make your acquaintance.' He clicked his heels together and bowed his head slightly. 'You requested my presence this afternoon?'

'Did you deliver a letter to me, yesterday, addressed to me personally,' Isabella enquired.

'Yes, I did,' Isham replied. Unusually for him, he felt slightly ill at ease in the presence of this woman. Her beauty was more striking close to than it was from across the room when he had seen her on board the *Pride of Probity* the other evening. Yet, equally disarming, was her direct manner.

'Did you write this letter, Mr Grisham?'

'No,' he replied. 'It was not in my hand.'

'In that case, may I be as bold as to ask whether you were aware of or had read its content?' Isabella sensed his discomfort at her barrage of questions.

'No, ma'am, I was not. I am not in the habit of reading other people's mail.'

'So, you were delivering the letter on behalf of another?' Isabella decided to continue her questioning unabated and press home her advantage.

'Well, not exactly,' Isham Griffen replied, irritated at being forced to give such an ambiguous answer but grateful for the natural pause in proceedings it gave him to give a more considered and specific response.

'You see, I found it down the side of the seat in the stage-coach. The stage that ferries people between here and the quayside,' he added for greater clarity. 'It must have fallen out of the bag or pocket of a previous occupant. I saw it was addressed to you and if I may be so bold, Mrs Rainecourt, it afforded me an opportunity to make your acquaintance.' Isabella felt her advantage slipping.

'And why would you want to do that?' she asked in as haughty a tone as she could manage.

'Because of my work,' he replied in a matter of fact way. 'I, Isham Griffen, am the chief project construction engineer for the Ravine River Railroad Company.' He felt into his waistcoat pocket and produced a business card containing his details. Feeling it inappropriate to thrust it at her, he placed it on top of the grand piano near the door. Isabella walked forward, picked it up from the shiny surface of the piano lid and read it. Isham Griffen was back in his preferred position again: that of being in control.

'Would you like afternoon tea, Mr Griffen?' she asked.

'That would be delightful, thank you Mrs Rainecourt.' Isabella symbolically conceded defeat for what she considered to be the first round of her interactions with Isham Griffen and rang the bell for her maid.

'Would you bring us afternoon tea, please, Eleanor', Isabella asked the maid as she entered the room, 'and place it on the table by the window. I am sure that Mr Griffen would appreciate the beauty of the view,' she said, turning politely to her guest.

'Yes, thank you ma'am.' The maid gave a slight curtsy before leaving the room.

*

'Talking of beauty,' Isham Griffen said, picking up on a thread of previous conversation that he could use to divert their small talk away from where he suspected Isabella Rainecourt might want to take it. 'Do you play?' He looked at the grand piano in the corner by the door.

'Yes,' she replied. 'I'd like to play everyday day but time doesn't always permit. I play most days, however. Mainly Chopin but a little Mozart and Bach.'

'I suspect you play beautifully.' Isabella chose to say nothing but smiled at her guest to acknowledge the compliment.

'Do you play?' she asked as she poured the tea.

'No, I'm afraid I don't,' Isham advised his host, 'but as an engineer I am fascinated by what I call the mathematics of music. The timing of notes, and that the time signature advises a musician anywhere in the world what rhythm to play, so that wherever the piece is performed and no matter by who, it is recognizable as the same.'

Isabella took advantage of her guest's brief monologue to serve tea. 'I suspect we have a number of areas in common, you and I,' he continued, 'and understanding the emergence of beauty from order is one of them.'

'And how do you deduce that, Mr Griffen?' Isabella asked, fascinated that this man who had probably come to destroy the peace and harmony of the community she had created could conclude that they might possibly have anything in common.

'I know I have only just met you but I am obviously aware of the impact you have had in this town, and I can also tell from your demeanour and the way you have organized your home. I apologize if that sounds very direct, but please take it as the compliment it is meant to be. I suspect you and I are all about an unshakable belief in standards and principles, Mrs Rainecourt. Some may accuse us of being too judgemental but what many don't appreciate is that judgement comes easy to us, as we have standards and principles with which we can compare.'

'You are very insightful, Mr Griffen,' Isabella said. 'Yes, I can see some of me in what you say,' she lied, underplaying just how accurate her guest's analysis was. She felt as if he was peeling her personality from her, layer by layer.

'And what about your boss, Burrell Challener?' Isabella, asked deciding that it was time to close the dance of small talk and tackle the big issue. 'Does he think in the same way that we do and, like me, appreciate the beauty that has emerged from the standards and principles we have established here in Probity. Or would he agree with Probity's critics that it is too divisive: the haves and have nots? Probity is welcome to all, of course, provided they are prepared to behave according to specified standards and principles. The law of the United States is based on exactly the same foundation. However, as Probity is limited in terms of space, we need to resort to the laws of capitalism, just like elsewhere, to ultimately decide who has the financial means to support themselves living here.'

'Exactly, Mrs Rainecourt!' Isham exclaimed. 'I agree with you entirely. In fact, I find it difficult to find fault with your logic and analysis. But I'm afraid Mr Challener doesn't think in the same way as us. He has a different view of the world and how it works. You see, he is very achievement orientated but not in a perfectionist way, like you with your town and me with the construction of my railroads, which I design to run at maximum efficiency. No, Burrell Challener just wants to be the winner. Even if it's a race of rats, he will have achieved in his eyes, provided he wins. One of the issues with people motivated in such a way is that they can be, how shall we say, pragmatic and bend the rules to gain advantage. But as we are both aware, Mrs Rainecourt, none of us are perfect – apparently. A saying, which by definition must include you and I.' Isabella smiled at her guest's cynical humour.

'So, would Mr Challener's idea of winning in terms of running a railroad mean building the longest, the one with the most coaches, the fastest, or the largest coverage?' Isabella asked.

'Ah, no, not exactly,' Isham Griffen replied. 'It's a good observation, however, on your part and will bring us neatly to the nub of our conversation. For Mr Challener, running a railroad is just a means and there is little point in winning just the means if you don't win the end result, which the means are designed to deliver.'

'And they are?' Isabella asked.

'Making money from the land speculation that rail routes offer. If he could do that without actually having to run trains along his roads, he would. I have never spoken to him about it, and neither would I, but in short I suspect Mr Challener would articulate his idea of winning as being the richest rail-road speculator.'

'I thought you might say that,' Isabella said quietly but firmly. 'Well, he might try and compete with my husband's steamboat business but there is little opportunity for land speculation in these parts, especially here in Probity. Property here certainly isn't cheap but the demand here is not great either and this is reflected in the price. May I ask, Mr Griffen? Where do you stand on this issue?'

'As regards Mr Challener, my position is neutral. I am not a permanent employee of his. I have been hired on a contract to construct the road. The overall route of the road to here and away from here is pretty much decided but not whether it should specifically run through Probity itself or around it. I have yet to finish my surveys and there is no guarantee that

Mr Challener will accept any recommendation that I make.'
Isabella swallowed hard. She knew this could end up turning
into a war.

'Again, Mrs Rainecourt, you make a worthy point about
the property values being limited by demand. But it depends
which way you look at it, and unfortunately at the moment, I
understand that Mr Challener looks at it a different way. You
may see Probity as a small, little-known oasis in a visually
beautiful but largely barren, economic landscape. Mr
Challener sees it as a booming railroad town, with many commercial opportunities, attracting a much larger population.
You may see the quayside as, out of necessity, a temporary
resting place for drunkards and womanisers, whereas he sees
it becoming an exclusive, small luxury resort at the water's
edge.'

'I see, Mr Griffen,' Isabella said solemnly. 'Well, clearly
there is a wide difference of opinion here and I am not sure
as to where we go next to resolve it.'

'I will certainly keep your concerns at the foremost of my
mind as I work on my surveys and see if it is possible to
accommodate your wishes, but in the meanwhile I suggest
you and I continue to converse. I thank you for your tea and
your time, Mrs Rainecourt,' Isham Griffen said as he stood
up to leave.

'Thank you, Mr Griffen. I will contact you again, shortly.'

'Eleanor,' Isabella said. 'I have written this note.' She passed
the maid a folded sheet of paper. Would you see it is delivered to the telegraph office and wired, please? It is urgent, so
I would appreciate it if you would make it a priority.'

'Yes certainly, ma'am,' Eleanor said in an obliging tone,
taking the note from her mistress. She noticed that it was
addressed to, 'Bose Hendry'.

CHAPTER 6

Bose Hendry rode along the top of the escarpment. It had been nearly a month since the Ravine River Railroad Company had been granted their charter but in that time they had managed to make significant changes to the landscape along the proposed route for their new railroad. Gangs of labourers were preparing the track bed, which was snaking its way over the hills, and at the point where Hendry stopped to take everything in, it hugged the escarpment fairly close to the edge, with dramatic views of the Ravine River below, before approaching the outskirts of Probity.

He was probably at the proposed road's highest point here and, looking through the lens of his brass telescope, he could make out a 'hell on wheels' tent city, which housed the workers and provided them with the excesses of refreshment and entertainment that seemed to motivate them. He estimated it would probably be six weeks or so before it reached Probity. Although life in these tent towns was of a feral nature in the evenings, their guests, the railroad builders, were a well-drilled army in the daytimes.

It was the graders who, with the aid of heavy steel ploughs drawn by oxen and the more basic pick and shovel cut, filled and prepared the track bed, followed by the track layers, who every thirty seconds would drop from a wagon two lengths of parallel line onto the ties that straddled the bed. Working in harmony with them were the measurers, who checked the rails were parallel with a rod, and the spikers, who dropped the spikes in position ready for the gangs to hammer in. As a consequence, the track laying was able to proceed at a fast walking pace.

Every so often, the continuous drone of men working was interrupted by the sound of an explosion cutting through the rock to create a path for the road to follow. Mules and oxen dragged wagons of gravel and stone used for track ballast from a quarry near the top of the escarpment. Impressed by the ability of human beings to organize themselves to work together in an efficient manner to achieve an otherwise impossible goal, Bose Hendry decided to move on and take a look at the quarry. Once the railroad was finished the forests that had been cut down to make wooden ties and provide wood for fuel would eventually grow back again and even the road itself, if not successful, would be left to rust and rot away, eventually disappearing into the ground. It was the quarry that was most likely to be the permanent addition to the landscape; no one was going to have the time or inclination to want to fill that back in again.

'Put your hands in the air, mister!' Bose Hendry pulled away from the edge of the quarry, turning his horse around as he did so. 'I said put 'em in the air, mister!' Hendry stared at the two men who were standing at the top of a pile of loose gravel. One of them had his Winchester rifle pointed firmly at Hendry's body.

'I'll leave them here, if you don't mind,' Hendry replied. 'On my horse's neck. You can see that he's nervous. When he gets like this he might rise up and frighten you into pullin' that trigger. Then I'll have to shoot you!' The man with the rifle looked angry. His companion placed his hand on his shoulder to calm him down.

'What you doin' up here, mister? This is private land.'

'I ain't seen no notices to that effect,' Hendry replied. 'Who says so?'

'I do. I'm head of security for the railroad.'

'Yeah, I know who you are,' Bose Hendry said, interrupting him. 'You're Carew Langdon, ain't yer. Just been released from jail.'

'How do yer know that, mister?' Langdon asked. His companion shifted his stance on the gravel slightly while still pointing his rifle at Hendry.

'Make it my business to know these things. As an ex lawman, sometime bounty hunter and security advisor myself, I would do. It's all part of my stock in trade.'

'There ain't no bounty on my head, mister,' Langdon was quick to point out. 'I'm goin' straight now. What's your name, anyway?'

'Hendry,' Bose Hendry replied.

'Hendry,' Langdon repeated. 'Huh. That's it, is it? Just Hendry? Ain't you got no forename?'

'Yes, it's Mister.'

'Is that it? Mister? Mister Hendry?'

'Yes, that's it. To you, my name is Mister Hendry.' Langdon's companion, feeling uncomfortable that his boss was being made a fool of and tied physically due to standing at a slant on loose gravel, shifted his feet again. Bose Hendry choose to read it as a sign of provocation, slid his right hand off his horse's neck, pulled his revolver from its holster and fired three shots into the gravel at the men's feet. Losing their balance, Langdon and his companion slid down the gravel and landed on their backsides by the feet of Bose Hendry's horse.

'You ain't no security advisor!' Carew Langdon said angrily, looking up at the man on horseback before him.

'Oh no? I actually am,' Hendry replied. 'And my advice to you two on this occasion is never level a gun at someone with intent to use it if you are not standing on firm ground or seated in a firm position. Good day, gentleman.' He touched the brim of his hat with his left hand and then rode away.

'I will show you the letter,' Isabella said, pleased to able to share it with someone she knew and trusted. She walked over to the bureau, retrieved it from the top drawer and passed it to Bose. He looked at the handwriting on the front and then turned it over and studied the seal on the back.

'So Griffen told you he was unaware of the contents, is that right?' Bose asked.

'Yes,' said Isabella. 'The sealing wax on the back looks too neat to have been tampered with before he gave it to me.'

'I suppose he could have easily written it himself,' Bose said, 'but we can check that by comparing it with his normal handwriting. Let me see what it says.' He looked with surprise, as he read the note's content:

Dear Mrs Rainecourt,
I do not wish to upset or offend you and neither do I wish to pry but I thought you ought to be made aware that your husband Hilliard is having regular intimate relations with one of the quayside whores.

'Do you think it is true?' Bose asked.

'Well, I don't know what to think?' Isabella replied. 'There is nothing in my husband's behaviour and relations towards me that would even suggest it could be but, on the other hand, he is a man of the world and could have a wider appetite for such activity than I do and chooses not to trouble me with it. Although, it is upsetting – very upsetting if it turned out to be true – as you no doubt know, us ladies tend to turn a blind eye to such dalliances as long we are still supported and provided for and our dignity respected.'

'It is interesting to appear to be so concerned about your welfare yet not brave enough to have signed it.'

'What do you mean?' Isabella asked.

'Well, it could be part of a deliberate strategy to unsettle you and your husband by Challener and his railroad. An attempt to make you anxious by filling your life with uncertainty in every quarter, weakening your resolve for a fight.'

'You think it's going to come to that?'

'I think it could do. Challener has already hired some outlaws to manage his security. That is not a good sign. You wouldn't normally hire those kind of people for that type of work. It is interesting also that Isham Griffen has offered himself as a potential benefactor so soon. All these events could just be coincidence, and I don't want to frighten you, but they could also be interrelated and part of an intricate plot.'

'I understand,' said Isabella, feeling a little overwhelmed.

'What do you want the scope of my brief to be, Isabella?'

'Well, at the moment, I feel that someone or a group of people are out to harm the Rainecourt family and business. This sounds so much more than an issue of just commercial competition. I would like you to investigate if this is the case, who is involved, what they intend to do and work out how we can stop them and protect ourselves. I will pay you handsomely for your endeavours.'

'Don't worry,' Bose reassured her. 'We will get to the bottom of it. I will start straight away. Don't tell anyone you have hired me, or what for. That could make you more of a target than you need to be. We don't want anyone to connect our pasts. As far as everyone else is concerned, I am a bounty hunter, sniffing around, looking for work. People will understand. Wherever there is opposition to a new railroad being built there is likely to be trouble sooner or later, often giving rise to feuds between warring factions. Normally more than any sheriff has got the time to handle. I've turned up in Probity just biding my time, waiting for it to break out.'

'OK, Bose,' Isabella said. 'I agree.'

CHAPTER 7

Bose Hendry's intuition told him that Isham Griffen was potentially a double dealer. Why would he want to try and impress Mrs Rainecourt that he might have some sort of sway over Burrell Challener's decision about whether the railroad ran through Probity or not? He was, no doubt, a highly paid contractor but one of the benefits of such employment was that it enabled the job holder to absent themselves from the internal politics of an organisation and, basically, take the money and run. There was no need for a location engineer to go out of his way to 'make the acquaintance' of a key opponent of a new railroad route. Most of those in his profession would prefer to get as far away from such people as possible to avoid any pressure or suspicion of falsifying their findings. He decided to make some discreet enquiries.

'How often do you clean out these coaches?' Bose asked the ticket seller as he bought a ticket for the ride down to the quayside.

'If you are sayin' they ain't clean enough for you, mister, I'll get someone to attend to it.'

'No, not at all,' Bose replied. 'I'm sayin' the opposite. They look immaculate.'

'Ah, thank you, sir,' the ticket seller said, changing his

tune. 'We inspect them after every ride and clean out any rubbish or lost property there and then.'

'What if someone left a letter by mistake down the side of the seat?' Bose asked.

'We would find it, sir. Funnily enough, that's the place we find most things, from wallets to watches, ladies' expensive earrings. I hope you haven't lost a letter, sir but if it was on one of our rides we would have found it and nothing has been handed in. No, we're very thorough sir. You'd be surprised what people lose, though. Why, we even lost two passengers the other night!'

'Oh?' said Bose interested in where this story was going.

'Yes, sir. On the 11.30pm from the quayside up to the top here. Two men got in at the bottom but when the stage reached the top here there was no one in it. It's bizarre, as if they had disappeared into thin air. The driver says he'd recognize one of 'em if he saw him again but there's been no sightings. Anyway, your ride is ready to descend now, sir.'

When he arrived at the quayside, Hendry alighted from the stagecoach and strolled along the front. One way was just boat houses, but when he walked the other way he found the main terrace of several double-storey buildings that housed a mix of shops, bars and restaurants. At the end of the quay, he discovered a narrow alleyway leading into a small, red light area with a gambling hall at the back of the bars and shops. The alleyway appeared to be the only way in and way out. In some ways the set-up was quite discreet: it was separated from the quayside where most people would congregate but standing at the entrance to the alleyway was an obvious spot for blackmailers to hang out and identify possible victims.

Bose Hendry went and sat outside a small bar overlooking the river and ordered himself a whiskey. Was the person who wrote the letter to Isabella informing her of her husband's supposed marital indiscretion a cuckold who wanted Isabella's help to win his partner back from her husband's clutches? Or was their motive more mercenary and they wanted Isabella to buy their silence and avoid the threat of public humiliation? Then there was Isham Griffen's odd claim that he had found the letter on the stagecoach. Yet according to the stagecoach staff this was not possible. Things did not seem to make much sense at the moment.

Perplexed, Bose put down his glass and allowed his attention to wander to the *Pride of Probity*, which was pulling alongside. He marvelled at the spectacle of this magnificent vessel, which could crush a man to death if he fell overboard between the quay and the boat, glide across the river and gently kiss its evening mooring as if they were lovers. He was amazed at its size and how many people it carried. He watched with interest as they walked down the gangplanks and onto the quayside. For many the boat was just a means for transporting freight to purchasers and travelling the river, but others saw it as a pleasure palace, where they could eat and drink, play cards, and even spend the night.

'Got it!' Bose suddenly exclaimed to himself. He grabbed his partly finished bottle of whiskey and strode towards the paddle steamer. After the last person leaving the vessel had vacated the gangplank, he went on board. Quickly finding the purser's office, he purchased a modest cabin for the night including a ticket to ride for the next day. He chose one along the corridor from Hilliard Rainecourt's personal suite.

'That's a good choice,' the purser advised. 'Mr Rainecourt will be travelling with us tomorrow, so the staff will keep a special eye on that corridor to ensure standards are being met.'

'Does he travel regularly with you?' Bose Hendry asked by way of making conversation.

'At least once a week and often he stays overnight, usually on a Friday,' the purser replied. 'In addition to a bedroom and sitting room, his suite also has a small office. It enables Mr Rainecourt to continue his work while experiencing the conditions which us staff work under. The cleaning lady always arrives early on those days and cleans Mr Rainecourt's suite before he boards. I'll see that she doesn't disturb you, sir.'

'Thanks for your consideration, purser,' Bose Hendry said.

CHAPTER 8

Bose Hendry made sure that he awoke early that morning. Shortly after 6.30, he heard the chambermaid walking down the corridor. As soon as she had passed his cabin, he quietly opened the door and peered out, just as she entered Rainecourt's suite with her mop, dusters and bucket and broom. Bose had been proud of his theory about the location of Hilliard Rainecourt's supposed affair. To carry it on in the more conventional places such as the establishments of the quayside's red light district would have been far too risky. The chances of someone of Mr Rainecourt's stature being spotted entering such an establishment were very high, to the extent that it would have been a significant and continuing drain on his financial resources just to silence the rumour mill. Far better to indulge in such acts of intimacy where people would least expect it; right under their noses!

Who, apart from the warped, would think anything ill of the chambermaid doing her chores in Hilliard Rainecourt's rooms, even while he was there? Wedging his cabin door half open, so that he could hear any signs of movement, Bose sat on his bed and rolled himself a cigarette. At 7am, he heard someone else coming along the corridor. After they had gone past his room he peered round the doorway. It was Rainecourt himself. He seemed to go through the motions of unlocking the door of his suite.

It was an hour and a half later that the maid left the suite. She may well have spent all that time doing the dusting or even conversing with her boss on entirely innocent matters. If so, that was fine. Bose hoped for Isabella's sake that the note she had received was some sort of a prank and without foundation. He didn't bother to hide in his room but stood in the doorway as the maid walked past, with her eyes firmly fixed on the floor. Compared with Isabella, she was an extremely ordinary looking woman, not one to have turned a man's head. Maybe he had this figured out wrong. Five minutes later, Hilliard Rainecourt left his suite, locking the door behind him.

At quarter to nine, Bose went into the grand saloon to help himself to the buffet breakfast. Hilliard Rainecourt was there, holding court with a small group of dignitaries. Bose choose not to affect an introduction, content to keep a low profile and just observe the goings on. With the paddle steamer almost an hour into its journey downstream, Bose decided to walk around the main deck. Friday daytime clearly wasn't the time for pleasure seekers. The deck was virtually devoid of people apart from a handful of homesteaders taking livestock and produce to market. Today was a day for transporting freight, the staple of Rainecourt's business, the trade that the railroad was plotting to steal from him. The pleasure seeker trade started in the evening and would last throughout the weekend. It would be far more difficult to move around the decks then.

The steamer began to slow down as it approached its first port of call, a small hamlet several miles or so downstream from Probity. Bose Hendry went upstairs on to the hurricane deck to get a better view of the docking. He wasn't certain but he thought he saw what appeared to be a body washed up on the shore line. He ran down the stairs to the purser's office.

'How long we stopping for, purser?'

'Twenty minutes, sir. Going ashore?'

'I thought I saw a body in the water, as we were approaching, the quayside,' Bose replied. 'I reckon a small boat would be the only way to reach it.'

'Let me get hold of the captain, sir.'

The oarsman steadied the boat as they approached the body. The top half was resting on the surface of a rock by the water's edge but the legs were still dangling in the water. It was clear to the three people in the boat that the person was not only dead but from the marks on the body and the dangling limbs they had suffered some sort of fall, consistent with bouncing off a series of rocks. Bose and a member of the *Pride of Probity* crew loaded the broken body into the rowing boat.

'That's Challener, that is,' a woman standing on the quayside exclaimed as they carried the body ashore.

'Who, Tilly?' The purser asked the woman to repeat the name.

'Seth Challener,' she replied. 'No good, low life. Given me a lot of personal grief he has. Not surprised he's met with an accident. He slept on the boat the other night and stayed most of the following day,' she said, indicating the *Pride of Probity*. Bose recognized her as the chambermaid from earlier.

'That's right. I remember,' said the purser. 'Was supposed to stay another night but boasted that he had changed his mind and had booked a room for the night in the Probity Grand Hotel.'

'Can I be of assistance?' asked the local pastor arriving at the quayside. 'My goodness!' he exclaimed as he came closer.

'Poor fellow. He has taken a real beating. If someone can help me carry him to the chapel, I'll prepare him for burial later. In the meantime, I'll take the wagon into Probity and inform the sheriff. Not that he'll be able to do much, I'm sure.'

'I'll ride back with you if I may, pastor,' Bose said. 'Let me help you carry Mr Challener to the chapel.'

'I assume the deceased is related to the Challener who is building the railroad,' the pastor said to Bose as they rode along the stony track.

'Well, the railroad mogul did have one remaining brother called Seth. I've heard of him but I've never met him.'

'Maybe the railroad mogul should view the body to confirm that it is his brother?' the pastor suggested. 'Besides, he might be prepared to pay more than the normal rates for the burial. Every little helps, you know.'

'Sure,' Bose agreed. 'You think that Tilly could be wrong in her identification?'

'No, but if she is the sole identifier of whom the person is and there is some dispute about it after the burial, I'm afraid her testimony would not hold much credibility with many of the folk around here.'

'Oh, why would that be?' Bose asked.

'Tilly has a past. A few years ago we had an outbreak of smallpox in the hamlet in which her child and her husband died. Miraculously, Tilly survived but turned to the red-light area on the quayside at Probity to make her living. Mrs Rainecourt, however, since her arrival has promoted a great deal of charity work, not only in Probity but the surrounding environs as well, and one of her key areas of interest has been to help fallen women. The idea is to facilitate the transition from being a sporting lady to a more honourable profession and dignified lifestyle. Not all fallen women want to participate but Tilly was an early volunteer for the scheme.'

'And how is she making out?' Bose asked.

'Well, in many ways very well,' the pastor replied. 'She has regular work on the *Pride of Probity* as a maid and seems to be able to hold the job down.'

'And in other ways?' Bose enquired.

'In other ways,' the pastor answered, 'it is really difficult to say. You see, she seems to have more money than she's ever had. I am sure that Rainecourt's pay is generous but Tilly's lifestyle seems to be in excess of what a chambermaid could ever afford. She says that she earnt and saved a lot of money when she worked as a sporting lady and to celebrate her return to a normal way of life is spending some of it. Plausible, I suppose.'

'Yes, I suppose it is,' Bose agreed.

'You wan'ed to talk with me, mister?'

'Are you the driver of the 11.30pm stage from the quayside, a few nights ago when the two passengers had disappeared by the time you got to the top?' Bose asked.

'Yep, that's me.'

'Whiskey?'

'Don't mind if I do. Thanks, mister.' Bose ordered a bottle and two glasses.

'I understand from your ticket seller that you could describe one of 'em?'

'Yes, I could. It was a cold night and the other one was well wrapped up. Scarf and hat, you know, could only see the eyes.'

'Wanna tell me what the other one looked like?'

'Yes, mister. Pour me a drink and I will describe him to you.'

Bose left the stagecoach driver with the bottle of whiskey and made his way to the Probity Grand Hotel.

'I am trying to trace the whereabouts of a friend of mine, who I believe had booked in to stay here a few nights ago but may not have arrived.'

'Can you tell me the person's name?' the clerk in charge of the reception desk asked.

'Mr Seth Challener,' Bose replied. The clerk looked through his register.

'Yes, here he is. He checked in earlier in the day. See here's his signature.' Bose checked the signature against the handwriting in the letter Isham Griffen had sent to Isabella.

'Thanks,' Bose said.

'I'm afraid there is a small matter of your friend's bill. Even though he didn't stay here, I am afraid your friend's bill still needs to be settled. If you would be good enough to oblige, sir?'

'I'm afraid not,' Bose replied. 'You see, he was not that good a friend.'

Leaving the hotel, Bose made his way across the square and up the grass bank to the Rainecourts' residence, where he requested an audience with the lady of the house. Having checked her mistress's availability, Eleanor showed him into the drawing room.

'I have some news of which you need to be aware,' he explained to Isabella, 'It affects how you ensure you keep yourself safe when conducting your daily business in and around Probity.' Isabella beckoned him to sit with her at the table.

'Go on,' she said with a slight hint of concern on her voice.

'There appears to have been a murder in Probity within the last few days. A body was washed up downstream this morning. It was that of Seth Challener, the middle brother of Burrell Challener. From his injuries it looks like he either fell or was pushed down the cliff face into the river.'

'Why do you think it was murder and not just an accident,' Isabella asked. 'He could have been drunk and stumbled in the dark?'

'Well, the night before Isham Griffen delivered that threatening note to you, two men got into the 11.30 stage-coach for the ride up to Probity from the quayside. But when the stagecoach reached the top, it was empty. One of those men, from the driver's description was Seth Challener.'

'Did the driver recognize the other man, who presumably knows what actually happened?'

'No, but it looks like it was Isham Griffen. The letter addressed to you was written by Seth Challener. His signature in the hotel register and the handwriting in the letter match. Griffen claimed he found that letter down the side of the seat in the stagecoach.'

'But he could have found it much later on, such as the fol-lowing day, when he just happened to be riding the same stage?' Isabella argued, aware of the implications that this might have for her.

'Not according to the stagecoach company,' Bose replied. 'They claim that they religiously clean the stage after each journey. There are, of course, always alternative explanations but the least contrived would be that Griffen robbed Challener in the coach and in amongst the spoils was the letter. The fact that the second person was covered up, or masked against the cold, also implies a premeditated crime.'

'But why would anyone want to rob Seth Challener so vio-lently?' Isabella said thoughtfully. 'His brother, Hiram, barely spoke of him. I was left with the impression that he was a bit of a nobody and lived on the fringes and from small projects undertaken for the eldest brother on his railroad. Not really smart enough to hold a permanent job down, nor clever enough to make a living outside of the law.'

'Hmm. Those types are often gamblers,' Bose commented. 'He'd been staying on the *Pride of Probity* and boasted of cutting his stay short to move into the Grand, according to the purser.'

'Perhaps he was a cheat?' Isabella suggested half joking.

'And perhaps Isham Griffen was the person Challener cheated who took offence?' said Bose, building on Isabella's train of thought.

'I can't imagine Isham Griffen as a card player,' Isabella continued. 'He seems too upright, too logical in his thinking to want to risk money on a game of chance.'

'But that's what good card players do,' Bose pointed out. 'They are constantly calculating and recalculating the odds of winning as the cards fall and knowing what they hold in their hand. It's a mathematical approach that can still be trumped by luck but is much less likely to be, especially against a less experienced player. And as an exceptional engineer, as we are led to believe, Isham Griffen is probably an exceptional mathematician.'

'Our reasoning could all be wrong though, couldn't it?' Isabella asked.

'Yes, it could be,' Bose agreed, 'but the more we try and piece together a story of events based around the evidence we have, the more credible it sounds.'

'Leaving Isham Griffen very much as our prime suspect,' Isabella remarked. 'I will need to keep him at a safe distance.'

'Yes. That will be a judgement call on your part, I'm afraid, Isabella. Ironically, keeping a potential enemy at a safe distance sometimes means keeping them close rather than far away.'

'I will use my intuition, Bose. Do you have any news of my husband's supposed infidelity?'

'Nothing of any note,' Bose replied, not wishing to worry

Isabella any more with what at the moment was still very much conjecture.

'All the women in these parts are suspects then as regards that matter,' she said, trying to make light of her situation.

'Or innocent,' Bose pointed out, finishing the conversation on a positive note.

CHAPTER 9

'Yes, it was Seth, all right,' Burrell Challener said to his chief finance officer. 'He looked a bit the worse for wear, badly battered and bruised, but it was him all right.'

'You sure he was killed,' the chief finance officer asked, 'and not had an accident such as a drunken fall.'

'Yep, the doc's been out of town but he's back now and came with me this morning. It was the first time we'd both seen the body. He confirmed it was murder. There were strangulation marks around Seth's neck.' He paused to draw on his cigar. 'You need to find some spare money in the books. I wanna put up a reward for the capture of his killer – dead or alive.'

'We can't really justify that. Not from the company accounts. How much were you thinking of?'

'I dunno,' Burrell replied, thinking what the capture of his brother's killer was worth in terms over and above revenge. 'Say $750 to start with, if the killer is found dead or alive, possibly rising to a maximum of $1,000 depending what further information is provided about the killer's motive.'

'That's a big sum of money,' the chief finance officer said, privately thinking to himself that neither of Burrell Challener's brothers had been worth even a dollar when they were alive. 'Really that should come from for your private resources. I know Seth, God rest his soul, sometimes worked for us but at the time of his death he wasn't on our payroll.'

'Yes, he was,' Burrell said sharply, correcting his colleague's statement. 'He was working for me. He was trying to find any information that indicated some sort of flaw or vulnerability in the Rainecourts' make-up. Something that might give the company leverage in negotiating a buyout of their steamboat company. The Rainecourts are very proud and honourable people. If their public credibility is destroyed, their appetite to fight will be undermined and then they will definitely lose. No one likes the skeletons in their closet being paraded in public.'

'Oh,' said the chief finance officer, sounding surprised. 'With all due respect, I never realised that your brother was capable of such detective work.'

'Well, you might think that,' said Burrell, 'but Seth did have some useful skills in that he was a good cheat, sneak and petty thief. He was also very underhand. In fact, I always thought he had the potential to make a living as a blackmailer but, of course, we'll never know that now. He sent me a telegram several days ago saying that he had come across what could only be described as hot news and was starting to act on it. He said he'd explain when he next saw me.'

'And he died before you were able to meet?'

'That's right,' Burrell replied. 'I'd love to know what he'd found out and what action he was taking.'

'It's still a lot of money for a reward,' the chief finance officer remarked, 'for someone who might turn out to embarrass the company if he had been doing something on its behalf that turned out to be illegal.'

'I'm not worried about any legality issues,' Burrell said in a dismissive tone. 'Don't get me wrong, I believe in law and order as much as the next man. You can't run a railroad without order and some rules. We also need to set boundaries with consequences for crossing them as a disincentive to stop people like my idiot kid brother thinking that they can behave with total impunity. Mind you, Hiram was a complete no-hoper. You see, in times of extreme technological and social change, like we've been experiencing since the Civil War, it can be difficult for the law to keep up and give codified guidance. As a consequence, it loses its relevance and the world ain't gonna stop because of it. People gonna find ways around it, by bending the rules a bit, ignoring them, or makin' up their own. Seth was very much at home operating under such conditions.'

'So, who do you think may have wanted to kill him?' the chief finance officer asked. 'It sounds like he may have found out too much.'

'I dunno,' Burrell replied. 'Perhaps it was one of the Rainecourts, or someone acting on their behalf. I wouldn't put it past that Hilliard to hire the person you would least suspect. And by the way, the likely assassin is not always a gunslinger from out of town: in a small place like this, those type of men stand out too much. What if my cheating snide of a brother had actually found something big on Hilliard, for example, and Rainecourt wanted to hush it up? I wouldn't put it past Hilliard to have him discreetly killed.

'You mean, made to look like an accident?'

'Yes, that's right. I wouldn't even put it past Hilliard Rainecourt to have his own wife done away with, if it got him out of a tight spot. That's the sort of person we are dealing with, you know.'

'I can't believe that,' said the chief finance officer, quite shocked. 'Not that beautiful, young trophy wife of his. He thinks the world of her.'

'You see,' Burrell interjected. 'You used the key phrase there: trophy wife. It might be hard for a man to dispatch his wife but a lot easier if she's really just a trophy.' He stubbed out his cigar in the ashtray with an emphatic gesture, as if to reinforce his point.

'A reward of the size you suggest should at least attract someone competent enough to find your brother's killer,' the chief finance officer said thoughtfully. 'Rumour has it that there is someone in town of that nature already. A stranger called Bose Hendry. Ex lawman turned bounty hunter, looking for work.'

'Well, it might be Mr Hendry's lucky day then, mightn't it. It certainly will be if he delivers my brother's killer to me.'

'Yes,' the chief finance officer agreed. 'It will be if he's any good. Have you heard of him?'

'No,' Burrell Challener replied, 'but I don't know any lawmen. Never have. If you want to influence the law and have it on your side so to speak, you don't deal with lawmen. You go much higher up the food chain, starting at senator level. Why do you think Senator Godefroy is one of our friends?'

'I know,' said the chief finance officer, resigned to having to carry out his boss's bidding. 'So how do you want me to account for the reward money?' the chief finance officer asked.

'Put it under, security expenses.'

'Should your head of security be made aware of this expense?'

'I don't particularly care,' Burrell said, shrugging his shoulders. He wondered why his directors felt the need to ask him everything when he had fully empowered them to make the majority of these types of decisions themselves. 'But just to be clear, I gave Carew Langdon the title of Head of Security to make him feel good about himself. In actual fact, Langdon's role only covers day-to-day security operations. He isn't in overall charge and couldn't be because he doesn't have the ability to make strategic security decisions, such as offering reward money when it is in the company's best interest to ensure that certain law breakers are brought to justice. That's my job.'

Carew Langdon and his gang met once a day in work time to catch up with each other and discuss what was going on in their new world of railroad security. They met in the caboose that sat behind Burrell Challener's personal railcar at the end of the road. Every day, an engine pulled this small ensemble forward on the few miles of new track that had been laid the previous day. The inside of the caboose was in sharp contrast to Challener's car. There were no brass or porcelain ornaments, leather sofas, hand woven carpets or other opulent fittings. But for a gang of five ex-outlaws who were more at home drinking cups of black coffee, chewing tobacco and then spitting it out onto the wooden floor, it served its purpose very well.

'Well boys,' said Carew, 'how you finding it, working on the right side of the law?' There were a few grunts and one OK. He understood what that was shorthand for. It meant that they found it damned boring. He felt the same. With a large amount of land to cover, they had to split it into five patches, with each man responsible for his own area. Burrell Challener was always more interested in knowing what was going on rather than having his security team deal with any trouble straight away, especially if that meant leaving another part of his construction site unpoliced. As long as they had good information to act on, it was easy to get a posse together and track down the miscreants. Working on their own for long periods of time could be lonely too but all the members of the Langdon gang had spent time in prison and had learnt how to handle that.

Being a member of a gang of outlaws, however, was quite

different. Most of the time, when they were working, the gang were together either planning a robbery or executing it and making a getaway. Then there was the social side: the banter, the drinking, the gambling and the team bonding. But there was nothing quite like the highs and adrenalin rushes of robbery day. From the silence at breakfast with each man sat there lost in his own thoughts as if his colleagues were complete strangers, to the hour or so of quiet relaxation and contemplation before the break-in, interrupted only by some mild banter and the occasional clinking of whiskey glasses. Nothing compared, however, to the feeling of absolute power and control of the actual robbery, itself, with frightened people offering, willingly – urging in fact – the masked, anonymous men before them to steal their prized possessions and get rich quick, at their victims' expense.

Finally, came what could be the biggest adrenalin rush of the day – the getaway. It certainly was if someone was chasing after them. However, once in the clear and as their emotions and physical reactions returned to normal, their minds would replay the things that went well and downplay those that didn't, as they began to prepare for celebration.

Carew Langdon missed those highs and lows and he knew that his boys did, too. The only activity in living life within the law that came anywhere close to imitating some of those highs and lows was gambling. But each member of the gang regarded themselves as better outlaws than gamblers. That was why he felt pleased, excited even, to share his news. 'Listen, boys,' he exclaimed, 'Mr Challener has given us the chance to earn some extra cash. Not an insignificant amount either. Minimum of $150 each but. . . .' he said pausing for effect, 'it could be as much as two hundred dollars! Interested?'

'Go on, boss,' said Smokey as the other gang members

murmured their approval. 'Someone has killed Burrell Challener's brother, Seth. Challener is pretty sure it is someone in the Probity community, not an outsider. The money is on offer to whoever can catch this person and help Mr Challener bring them to justice. What d'yer say?'

'Sounds good so far, boss.'

'Yeah. Are there any conditions?'

'Good question, Smokey,' said Carew, revelling in his leadership role. 'Only one really. He doesn't want us to neglect our day jobs, to go scouring for his brother's killer. The security of the railroad construction site is of paramount importance. But Mr Challener believes that our skills and knowledge could have an important part to play in bringing the killer to justice. So I suggest that we operate as a team, like the old days. If one of us gets a lead and needs help in pursuing it, others of us will have to cover the vacated areas. Remember, the bar staff in all the best saloons you've ever visited operate on this basis.'

'We get it, boss,' said Smokey. 'Where do we start?'

'A couple of us met the arrogant Bose Hendry the other day. A newcomer in town. Bounty hunter. With all due respect to the man, I think he is smart: capable of finding the murderer. But he is not as smart as us. I suggest we keep an eye on Mr Hendry and let him lead us to the killer!'

As an engineer, Isham Griffen was not prone to believe in or willing to respond to moments of intuition. In fact, he would have argued quite rigorously that such concepts had no scientific foundation and as a consequence were just a form of superstition: the mind's way of 'tossing a coin' to prevent the indecisive from becoming paralysed by their own indecision. He was surprised therefore to start waking up one morning with a picture in his mind of a law man called Bose talking with Isham's uncle, who engineered the construction of a number of railroads for the cattle towns.

That in itself, did not particularly bother him. After the shock announcement of the murder of Burrell Challener's brother, the name Bose Hendry was on the lips of many of the construction site workers. For some, the arrival of a bounty hunter in town, a maverick, hanging around waiting to see if a criminal or bail jumper needed hunting down in return for money was quite a romantic notion but Isham Griffen was not one of those. He was totally indifferent about such men. What surprised Isham, therefore, was not that he should dream about one, but once fully awake that he should resolve to investigate this dream further. It was as if the dream was an indication that something was troubling him and asking for resolution, but he could not work out what it was.

Isham's intellectual powers rarely let him down, which was why he put so much store in them. By lunchtime his trust had been rewarded, or at least in part, with his memory being able to shed more light on the issue. He recalled his uncle telling him tales from his actual experience of the Wild West and one of them was about a remarkable lawman called Bose Hendry. He remembered his uncle saying that some of the feats of this man left those of better known lawmen whose heroics were popularised by dime store novelists in the shade. But Isham still felt troubled. There was still something missing, the sense and purpose of this whole episode were incomplete. Being paid by results, rather than by time spent, and under the pretext of urgent family business, Isham decided to visit some of the old cattle towns where his uncle had made his name as a railroad engineer. He would either find a logical explanation for this unusual situation or have to admit that even he had some neuroses.

Having arrived in Kansas by train, Isham Griffen changed to a branch line that took him west to a small country town.

Ever prepared, he had done his homework and was on his way to the home of a retired newspaper editor who during his career had worked for a number of key newspapers in the cattle towns. His calling card was that he was his uncle's nephew. He assumed rightly that his uncle had built up sufficient goodwill in his time in the area and that any member of the Griffen family would not be unwelcome. He also needed a good cover story for his visit, one that would get the old man talking freely about the past. A chance for the old-timer to show off his knowledge, in particular about Bose Hendry.

'Hello, Mr Reynolds, sir,' Isham said as he stepped up onto the veranda and shook the old man's hand. 'I'm Isham Griffen. My uncle was the engineer who constructed many of the railroads around these parts.'

'Pleased to meet you, Isham,' old man Reynolds said. 'Heard you'd be dropping by. I knew your uncle well. Fine man and a fine engineer. So, what can I do for you, son?'

'I was doing some research into the lawmen and heroes of the old cattle towns,' Isham lied. 'In my spare time I'm an avid reader of dime store novels about the Wild West,' he explained, keeping up the pretence. 'I wanted to find out how closely the heroes of these novels are modelled on the real lawmen whose actual activities and behaviours inspired the authors.'

'Ha, ha,' the old-timer chuckled. 'Well, I ain't read too many of them dime novels, young man but I sure know plenty about the actual sheriffs that ran the cattle towns, from first-hand experience as well. Here, son,' he said pushing a glass across the table towards Isham. 'Join me in a whiskey.'

For the next forty minutes, old man Reynolds regaled Isham with tales of derring-do committed by the various law breakers who frequented the cattle towns, and the lawmen who brought them to justice. 'So, you see, son. Those dime store heroes probably ain't too dissimilar from the men they were modelled on.'

'My uncle used to talk about Bose Hendry. Was he a great lawman? Did you know him?' Isham asked.

'Bose? Yes, I did,' the old man replied. 'Nowhere near as famous as the Earps and Mastersons but no less courageous or rigorous at enforcing the law. Bose wasn't worried about the lack of fame. Wasn't that kind of man. Had a distinct disliking for freeloaders, though. You wouldn't wanna get on the wrong side of him. Very clever man as well. He had a sharp mind. He'd have made a very good detective back east. He was responsible for catching the Hiram Challener gang. Hiram was the kid brother of one of the railroad builders around here and a nasty, vicious piece of work. The gang robbed a bank and Challener shot and killed the bank clerk. I covered the story myself.'

'How did Hendry catch them?' Isham asked.

'Well, it was a very badly planned robbery and being a novice at this game, Challener hadn't taken sufficient care securing his disguise. In the panic that immediately followed the shooting he was recognized by several witnesses.'

'Then what happened?'

'The gang had a hideout but Bose Hendry found it,'

'Through clever detective work?' Isham asked.

'I don't actually know, son, but he did. There was a rumour goin' around at the time that Bose persuaded Hiram's woman, Belle, to tell him where the hideout was. That's right. Belle Couer I think her full name was but she had dropped the surname and was just known as Belle. Some reckoned she was one of the de Courcy family on the eastern seaboard. If she was, she was a long way from home because that family had aristocratic blood in it. Real beauty though, Belle was. Anyway, on the day before her lover, Hiram, was hung, or so the story goes, Bose Hendry smuggled her out of town and Belle Couer or whatever her real name was, was never seen or heard of again.'

'Thanks, Mr Reynolds,' Isham said. 'Your stories are really fascinating. I've heard of the de Courcys by the way and you are right about them being descendants of the aristocracy. French aristocracy to be precise.'

On the train journey back to Probity, Isham Griffen was able to rationalize his dream. He now realised that it was his mind's way of giving him a warning sign that Bose Hendry was some sort of intellectual rival who might try and scupper his ambitions regarding Mrs Isabella Rainecourt's future.

CHAPTER 10

Bose Hendry sensed trouble. Big trouble. At some point Hilliard Rainecourt and Burrell Challener were going to clash. Two men who had conquered their part of the frontier to become wealthy were on a collision course, and neither of them were the type of man who would roll over and let the other one attack his empire without a fight. As the aggressor, Bose sensed that Challener and his railroad had the advantage. They would keep pushing ahead building their road until Hilliard Rainecourt attempted to stop them. The fact that Rainecourt appeared to have done nothing, apart from using reasoned argument to try and prevent the railroad being granted its charter, seemed odd. Hilliard must surely have some plan to deal with Challener but if so he was definitely playing it close to his chest and certainly hadn't shared it with his wife.

'I wouldn't expect him to do that,' Isabella explained to Bose. 'At times when I have tried to show an interest in the business side of the steamboat company, Hilliard has always said that I shouldn't bother my pretty head with such complexities. Just enjoy the pleasures which the company has afforded us, he always says to me.'

'I guess I'll just have to be patient for the time being,' Bose told her. 'I can't force the situation without having more information to go on. But sooner or later, something's gonna have to give.'

'Still no evidence of my husband's supposed infidelity?' Isabella asked.

'No,' Bose replied. 'I suggest that no news is good news.'

Indeed, the only motivation for still investigating whether Hilliard Rainecourt was engaged in any extra-marital activity was Bose's intuition. There was precious little evidence. He had spent a further two nights on the *Pride of Probity* and although he saw Tilly sweeping the deck on one occasion, there was no sign of Hilliard Rainecourt being on board. He had investigated the situation as inconspicuously as he could in order to ensure that Tilly was unaware that she was being spied on. What he was unaware of, however, was that other people were watching him.

Bose decided the time had come to either rule Tilly out of his investigation or keep her as a suspect and that the best way to do this without arousing her suspicions was to attempt to befriend her. The *Pride of Probity* was not the best place for such a social intervention and, given Tilly's past, probably not on the quayside either, so he decided to engineer a chance meeting in the hamlet where she lived.

'It has to be Rainecourt, Carew,' one of his gang members demanded.

'Why d'yer say, that?'

'Well, think about it. Mr Challener told us that his brother liked a game of cards. Seth had probably been playin' on the paddle steamer the night he died. Rainecourt couldn't believe his luck; the enemy walking into his lair, so he had him done away with, once Seth left the boat.'

'So, why would he wanna do that?' Carew Landon asked.

'Maybe Seth cheated him out of money,' the outlaw replied.

'Or, Seth's killin' was a warning to Mr Challener that he shouldn't mess with the Rainecourts,' one of the other outlaws suggested. 'He may not have done it personally but the order to carry out such an act could have only come from Rainecourt himself.'

'Do you think Hendry saw you on the *Pride of Probity*?' Langdon wanted to know.

' 'Course he did, boss. But he doesn't know us. He only knows you and Smokey from that altercation at the gravel pit. If he remembered us at all, it would have been just as members of the public.' His men seemed to have talked themselves into the belief that Hilliard Rainecourt had sanctioned Seth Challener's execution. He wasn't so sure himself.

'So, you think Hendry was out to get Rainecourt in order to claim Mr Challener's reward and that was why he was on the boat?'

'He had a cabin for two nights, the Thursday and the Friday. I saw it on the purser's log, boss. There are far cheaper places to stay in town.'

'He was definitely working. He was acting too furtively to be on a pleasure cruise. I saw him go to Rainecourt's suite a few times. He would knock, then try the door once or twice, which must have been locked because he would then put his ear against it to listen if there was someone inside. He was definitely after Rainecourt. He was expectin' him to turn up but the man never showed. Not while we were on the boat, anyway.'

'Fortunate that Rainecourt didn't because otherwise Hendry would have got to him before us and claimed the reward money.'

'I see,' Langdon said, starting to feel more confident that what he was being told, made sense. It certainly sounded like

Hendry was acting suspiciously as regards Rainecourt. It would be typical of the likes of Hendry to carry out an execution in someone's private quarters rather than in a public place; more professional that way. Yes, Langdon, thought to himself, it all adds up. To avoid any recriminations however, he thought Rainecourt's demise would need to look like an accident.

In order not to appear threatening or attract any undue attention, Bose decided to place his guns in his saddle-bag and leave his horse tied up behind the chapel. Taking a short cut to Main Street, through the graveyard, he was surprised to see Tilly sat on a bench with her head bowed, close to the main entrance of the chapel. She was clearly unaware of his presence and lost in her own thoughts. She appeared to be waiting for someone. Bose ducked down behind a tombstone and started to rearrange the flowers on the top of the grave, as if he was attending its upkeep – the long, lost friend of the grave's inhabitant paying his respects; a useful cover if Tilly or the man walking towards her should discover that their assignation may no longer be private.

'Shall we go inside the chapel?' the man asked. Bose knew from his voice that it wasn't Hilliard Rainecourt.

'No,' Tilly said firmly. 'You never know when the pastor is going to come in and suddenly creep up on you. It looks more like a chance meeting if we are here outside. Did you bring my money, Worth Godefroy?'

'Yes, I did. It is here.' He passed her a brown envelope. She tore it open and started to count the bills inside. 'It's all there,' the senator assured her. 'You don't need to check it out here.'

'Just making, sure, Senator,' Tilly said.

'I've always paid you on the nail for your services in the past,' the senator pointed out. 'How long is this going to go on for? I might be wealthy but I am not a bottomless pit of money.'

'You're a bank director, aren't you?' Tilly challenged. 'You can afford it. You can't afford not to, with what I know of your past and your personal preferences. It would never do for people to find out about what their elected representatives get up to in private, would it?'

'I thought you'd finished with all that, Tilly?'

'I have, Senator,' Tilly replied. 'I couldn't carry on working the street and indulge in kiss and tell. If word got around that I was doing that, I'd have soon had no customers.'

'Someone's put you up to this, haven't they?' Senator Godefroy asked angrily. 'It's that Burrell Challener, isn't it? The number of times I have put my reputation on the line for that man! He pays me for my loyalty on one hand and then takes it away with the other, by blackmailing me to ensure that I am never disloyal. He's, he's incorrigible.'

'Senator,' said Tilly raising her hand, 'I am my own woman. You of all people should know that. Always have been, always will be.' She saw he looked crestfallen. 'Don't worry. I don't plan to bleed you dry. Just need to get myself set up on a firmer footing in my new life, that's all,' she added, trying to show a small degree of empathy. 'But until then, a fortnight today, same place, same time, yes?'

'Yes, I suppose so,' the senator agreed reluctantly. Bose Hendry waited until they had left the graveyard before departing himself.

CHAPTER 11

Carew Langdon didn't call one of his gang Smokey for nothing. It wasn't anything to do with his heavy smoking habit, however. Smokey had earnt his nickname from his predilection for lighting fires and was a committed arsonist. Whether it was lighting sticks of dynamite to blast open bank vaults or knocking over oil lamps to set fire to people's property, it mattered not to Smokey. The rapid destruction of structures that had taxed man's ingenuity to design and exhausted his labour to build, held an almost childlike fascination for him. Of course, he could have put this predilection to a lawful and constructive use, such as railroad building: for example, dynamiting the stubborn rock faces that impeded the proposed path of the road. Unfortunately, that process was too disciplined and controlled for Smokey's liking.

Torching the *Pride of Probity* was far more suited to Smokey's appetite for practising his craft. He saw it as an honour that Carew Langdon had given him the responsibility for avenging the murder of Seth Challener and ensuring that justice was served by the supposed 'accidental' death of Hilliard Rainecourt. It would not only be a feather in his personal cap but would help give credence to the legend he and his colleagues were trying to create, that the Langdon gang were a force to be reckoned with.

Earlier on in the day, Smokey had made a reconnaissance of the paddle steamer during one of its stops. Under the guise of a maverick card player who was having a break from the tables and enjoying the comforts that the boat had to offer, Smokey was able to act the part with verve and panache. On the pretext of claiming that, as a successful man himself, he would enjoy the chance of meeting a fellow successful man, he was bold enough to ask the purser when Hilliard Rainecourt would next be on board. With no reason to suspect anything untoward, the purser gladly advised Smokey that Mr Rainecourt would not only board that evening but would be staying the night.

Pleased that he wouldn't have to wait long to achieve his mission, Smokey retired to a room he had rented in a quayside boarding house to prepare his next moves. His key decision centred on whether to go for a series of small, multiple fires that would stretch the crew's fire-fighting capacity, or go for just one, much larger fire. It didn't take Smokey long to realize that the latter would be the best choice, not least because it would enable him to use his fire lighter of choice: a stick of dynamite. Smokey knew also that steamboats had a poor record for exploding engines; the ideal cover for making what he had in mind later that evening look like an accident.

Bose Hendry sat on the quayside outside one of the bars enjoying a glass of whiskey in the early evening sunlight. After having eavesdropped the meeting between Tilly and Senator Godefroy in the graveyard, Bose decided not to talk with Tilly: not at this stage, anyway. Provoking a reaction was a high-risk strategy, in that she might clam up completely or even go on the offensive, and then he would have to watch his back even more. Far better if a suspect was to drop their guard and, unprovoked, give themselves away. From what he had overheard at the graveyard, Bose knew that Tilly certainly had something to give away and he was more likely to find out what this was if he waited until her next meeting with the senator, where he planned to be secretly present.

He was starting to surmise from their last rendezvous that Senator Godfrey's assumption that Burrell Challener was his blackmailer and acting through Tilly could well be wrong. What if Hilliard Rainecourt was the blackmailer acting through Tilly? If so, there may well have been clandestine meetings between the two of them, of which Seth Challener had become aware but had misread these liaisons, as extra-marital in nature. Although intrigued, Bose knew that patience was going to be a virtue in this situation and realized that, at least for now, the expedient course of action would be to sit tight and watch and wait.

In the peaceful atmosphere of an early summer's evening, it was difficult to feel impatient about anything. It seemed almost beyond comprehension that the elitists of the area were unmercifully plotting each other's downfall. The *Pride of Probity* had docked for the night and her commercial daytime passengers were disembarking, while the evening leisure crowd were assembling behind the boat's owner, Hilliard Rainecourt, and waiting to board.

It was among that latter group that Bose thought he spotted Smokey, who he recalled from his earlier altercation with Carew Langdon at the gravel pit. But if that particular Smokey had come across to Bose as a rough, coarse idiot, this one was a character transformed. Dressed in a smart pair of black suit trousers and a dress shirt, complete with bootlace tie and a satin waistcoat, he looked like charm personified, smiling at the other guests and doffing his hat to the ladies. Bose slowly rose to his feet to get a better view. He scanned the crowd to see if he could spot Carew Langdon but to no avail. Perhaps he had made a mistake and the charming man just looked like Smokey.

Bose took out his pocket telescope to check if his eyes had been deceiving him. Focusing the instrument on the man's face, he realized that they hadn't. It was definitely Smokey. The unkempt hair had been oiled and slicked back off the forehead, giving greater emphasis to the pointed nose and small narrow eyes. The cheroot hanging carelessly out the side of his mouth as he smiled added to the image that this was a seasoned, man of the world. He lowered the scope to Smokey's waist. There was no sign of a gunbelt. Perhaps Smokey had left the gang and found his true calling as a hustler, Bose wondered. As he lowered the scope some more, he saw that Smokey was carrying a small, rolled up oil cloth bag. Bose recognized it immediately. He had seen a number of them on the first day that he had ridden over Challener's railroad construction site. They had been being used to carry sticks of dynamite.

In the grand saloon, Smokey mingled into the thick of the crowd. His intuition told him that he was being followed. It had only been a half glance behind him at the people still waiting to board but at the end of that queue he was sure that he had spotted Bose Hendry. More importantly, he thought that Bose Hendry had spotted him. Smokey knew not to look back and make it appear that he was worried that someone was following him. Besides, he reasoned that it was a lot harder to recognize a man from behind. Provided he didn't feel a tap on his shoulder, he needed to casually make his way to the far side of the room and exit through one of the side doors. From there, he could quickly make his way to the small staircase that led down to the boiler room.

All he needed to do then was walk along the short corridor, light the fuse on the stick of dynamite, leave it on the floor outside the boiler room door, beat it back up the stairs and walk off the boat onto the quayside. The explosion itself wouldn't cause damage beyond repair; it was the ensuing outbreak of fires that would do that, but the time lapse between the explosion and the devouring, hot, hungry flames should mean that all but the unlucky few would be able to escape. Unfortunately, with his cabin on the deck over the boiler room, Hilliard Rainecourt was likely to be one of the unlucky few.

Bose Hendry waited patiently in the queue as he didn't want to create a panic. That would be a signal for Smokey to carry out quickly whatever exactly it was that he had planned and potentially make it easier for him to escape. Bose reasoned that Smokey wasn't on a suicide mission aiming to sink the boat and everybody on it. He saw Smokey as the sort of man who would want to escape and if he had ultimately been sent by Challener, it could be to temporarily disable the boat as a warning to the Rainecourt family to resist taking on his railroad company.

The delay in boarding, however, gave him a chance to figure out a strategy of what to do once on deck. Finally having boarded, he started to make his way to the stern of the paddle steamer, convinced that blowing the paddle wheel off the end of the boat would be the best way of disabling it, only to find his path blocked by the purser.

'Sorry, sir, but I see that you are carrying a firearm,' the purser said.

'So?' Bose challenged.

'Perhaps standing in the crowded boarding queue, you missed the notice, sir, advising that anyone carrying a firearm must leave it with the purser until they disembark or else they will be escorted from the boat.' Two heavy-looking deckhands appeared from the shadows.

'But I think someone has already boarded who wants to do harm to the boat.'

'I don't think so,' the purser said. 'They wouldn't have got through security here.'

'Not with a gun,' Bose said impatiently, 'but with dynamite.'

'Why would anyone want to do that?' the purser said in a bemused tone. 'Look sir, The ban on firearms is a new measure brought in today by Mr Rainecourt, which is why we have the pleasure of his company tonight. It is for a trial period only just while there are more people in the vicinity with the construction of the railroad. It is a precautionary measure to avoid any trouble, that's all. Now, are you going to oblige me by giving me your firearm or are you going to leave?' The two heavies moved closer.

'OK,' said Bose slamming his revolver down on the purser's desk. 'You can hang onto my gun.'

'Must be my lucky day,' Smokey muttered to himself. 'I must have given that no good critter Hendry the slip.' He unravelled the fuse wire and connected it to the stick of dynamite. Smokey then removed the bootlace tie from around his neck and used it to tie the stick of dynamite firmly to the boiler room door, to ensure that it would get blown off its hinges. Satisfied with his handywork, he puffed on his cheroot ready to light the end of the fuse.

It was the smell of the cheroot that alerted Bose Hendry to Smokey's presence. Damn it, he thought to himself. He's goin' for the boiler room! As he reached the top of the stairs, Bose's frame cast a shadow over Smokey at the end of the corridor. Smokey hastily untied the stick of dynamite from the door and held it in his hand.

'Damn you, Hendry!' Smokey exclaimed. Bose reached into his boot and pulled out a knife with an eight-inch blade.

'Interesting fight, cowboy,' Smokey said sarcastically, as he lit the fuse wire on the stick of explosive. 'A knife ain't no match against dynamite. Here catch.' Smokey tossed the dynamite up to Bose but slightly to one side. In trying to catch it, Bose Hendry unbalanced and fell down the side of the stairs. 'See you, sucker!' Smokey exclaimed and was off up the stairs. Bose picked himself up from the floor and, grabbing the stick of dynamite, cut off the lit end of the fuse with his knife and allowed it to burn itself out on the floor.

As he reached the top of the staircase, Bose was greeted by the smell of smoke and shouts of 'Fire! Fire!' Crowds of people were standing on the decks above, looking down at the large dancing flames emerging from a small area containing big bales of straw that had been stored on the open deck next to the boiler room. Through the swirling smoke Bose could just make out the fleeing figure of Smokey, the starter of the fires, running along the quayside. The bales had been bound with wire, so grabbing a boat hook, he pulled the two burning ones away from the rest to prevent the others from catching alight. Members of the crew arrived with fire buckets and, forming a human chain between the river and the bales of straw, soon managed to extinguish the fire, with water from the river.

The danger having receded, the crowd on the upper decks dispersed and returned to the pleasurable activities they had been engaged in, blissfully unaware as to how close they could have been to a painful and violent death. Only three people on board the *Pride of Probity* that evening appeared to have pre-empted such an outcome. One of course, was Bose Hendry, who while standing on the hurricane deck having a calming smoke and looking out over the river, spotted a small rowing boat. The second person was the man who was rowing the boat downstream, away from the paddle steamer. His strong, tireless strokes showed a determination to reach a stretch of flat bank on the other side as quickly as possible. Even through Bose's pocket telescope however, it was difficult to make out who the man was, as his face was obscured by the back of the third person, his passenger. At a guess, Bose thought the man could have been Hilliard Rainecourt. The passenger was sat still but upright in her seat, with her back towards the *Pride of Probity*. It was almost as if she didn't want anyone on the steamer to see who she was. If they had have done, locals would have recognized her instantly as Tilly.

CHAPTER 12

'I don't know if I am prepared to carry on like this, Tilly,' Senator Godefroy said in a frank tone as the two held their latest meeting in the graveyard. 'You're bleeding me dry. You may think I have a bottomless pit of money just because I am a bank director but what you fail to understand is that the privilege of being a bank director and also a senator is based more on ability and reputation than how much money one has.'

'So, what you really sayin', Senator? That you're prepared to gamble that I ain't gonna tell on you if you stop payin' me, or else just take the hit? Or are you gonna have me bumped off? A one-off payment to a hit man and no more worryin' about how much longer I'm gonna carry on extracting payments from you.'

'In accordance with my reputation, I have far too many scruples to have you assassinated,' the senator claimed with indignation. 'I thought you would have some as well, having put your old ways behind you.'

'I do but you have to appreciate I am in a transition period,' Tilly pointed out. 'When I worked the streets, I made a great deal of money but now, as a cleaner I earn a pittance by comparison. I need to build up a nest egg, which is what your payments are helping me do. If the wealthy want me to be virtuous and poor, they are expecting me to be better than they are and that don't seem right, somehow.'

'I can see you're reasoning,' said the senator empathetically. 'But why pick solely on me. I've done my bit. Pick on someone else. I have worked hard to get where I am. I wasn't born into money. That do-gooder, Isabella Rainecourt – it's all her fault. She hasn't thought through her scheme to reintegrate fallen ladies back into society properly!'

'Listen,' said Tilly. 'You and I can agree on that. It is bad luck that I picked on you but it was only because you were my wealthiest client. Anyway, I have an idea whereby we can help each other. One of the things you pick up on when working the streets is information: confidential information. Many clients tell you things they really shouldn't. Tryin' to make you think you're with somebody special, somebody really important rather than just some other loser. I have had a number of people come to me wantin' to buy certain types of information. Willin' to pay good money for it. Now, rather than give me money, you might have the information they want. You tell me an' I sell it to 'em without tellin' 'em where I got it from. How does that sound? Involves me in more work but it stops you from doin' something you might later regret, such as makin' me tell the world about your seedy secrets cos you won't pay me anymore cash.'

'What sort of confidential information?' the senator demanded to know.

'Well, I've had a number of people who I would term as speculators. Those who want to invest in bonds, for example. They would first need to know the content of Challener's railroad accounts, however. Not the fiction he publishes for public consumption but the other set of numbers: the real set. People have made a lot of money out of the railroads but some fear the bonanza might fast be coming to an end.'

'I can't possibly tell you what is in the accounts!' Senator

Godefroy exclaimed.

'No, of course you can't. I wouldn't expect you to do that!' Tilly reassured him. 'No. My clients would probably be interested in where they are being held. If they could get their hands on them, I am sure they would pay me handsomely for the privilege and then I should be able to leave you alone. So, what do you say?'

'OK. Here, look. I'll write the address down for you, now. I then want you to copy it onto your hand and give me back my original, which I will destroy.'

'All right,' said Tilly bemused. 'I am sure it would be easier just to tell me.'

'Even graveyards can have ears,' the senator replied.

'You're just paranoid,' Tilly said.

'Maybe, but life has made me that way.'

CHAPTER 13

'Well, Senator Godefroy, how is it?' Burrell Challener asked in a teasing way. He enjoyed mocking the senator, a man who was quick to see the difficulties in situations and view them as problems rather than challenges. It was particularly good sport, especially of late when the senator had happened to mention that he was starting to regard the whole world as being a conspiracy against him. 'Of course it is,' Burrell would rib him. 'That's the only reason we are here; to overcome the challenges put before us, to try and make the world a better place.'

'Huh!' the senator answered, not wishing to get involved in a philosophical discussion. 'If you like challenges, Burrell, then I can give you some.' Senator Godefroy knew that his next comments needed to be taken seriously and not punctuated by a series of jibes and quips from this arrogant railroad baron. As Burrell leaned back in his chair and sucked on his cigar, Worth Godefroy perched on the corner of Burrell's desk so that he could look down on his tormentor from a dominant position.

'Go on, Worth,' said Challener, correctly interpreting the signals. 'I'm listening.'

'I have it on good authority from my information sources that some investors are interested in laying their hands on the Ravine River Railroad Company's accounts. They are concerned that the versions released for public consumption are, how shall we say, a more optimistic view of the company's current position and its future.'

'What grounds could they possibly have for thinking that?' Burrell Challener asked. 'Do they honestly think we would be building this new road if our finances were not in a good state? You are our banker, what do you think?'

'It's not what I think, it's what the bank's board of directors think,' Worth said firmly.

'An' what's that?' Burrell asked. 'We've made a lot of money for your bank and for you privately, Senator Godefroy. Don't forget about that.'

'I know, we all thank you for that. But what worries the board is, for how much longer is that going to be the case? I do know that they will not be willing to advance the railroad any more money without reviewing the accounts. Technically, we should have done that more in the past, especially with some of the company's past financial difficulties, but as an act of good faith and indeed, sound financial judgement on our part, we decided to let it go. But not anymore.'

'So, you are saying the bank's view is not dissimilar to that of these investors?'

'That's right,' Worth Godefroy replied. 'The bank, I am sure of course, will take a more pragmatic attitude to any discrepancies there might be, certainly compared with individual investors who can become quite emotional about such matters.'

'Just out of interest,' Burrell said slowly as he studied the ash on the end of his cigar, 'an' I realize that you are probably not in a position to know who these individual investors are and tell me, but how deep do their concerns about the state of the accounts run?'

'I am glad you asked that question, Burrell,' the senator

replied. 'It's the one I wanted you to ask. It shows that you are taking me seriously. I would say that they would pay good money for someone to remove them for independent inspection.'

'I see,' said Burrell thoughtfully.

'You said we are put on this earth to deal with challenges,' Worth reminded him.

'I did,' Burrell replied, 'and you said you would give me some. But don't worry, they'll be dealt with.' He looked up and smiled at the senator, his eyes beaming with confidence.

'Bose,' Isabella said, taking his hand. 'I'd like to introduce you to my husband, Hilliard.'

'Sir,' said Bose shaking Hilliard's hand.

'Pleased to meet you, Bose. My wife has told me you're her one trusted friend from the past and that you have been helping and advising her on how to keep our community safe from the threats it potentially faces ever since Burrell Challener won his railroad charter.'

'Trying to help out where I can, sir,' Bose acknowledged modestly.

'Well, son, it's an honour to meet you, indeed it is,' Hilliard Rainecourt continued. 'I am particularly impressed with how you saved my paddle steamer the *Pride of Probity* and everyone on her from annihilation. A number of people on board saw what you did. It was heroic stuff. I, myself and one of my staff, Tilly, had to activate the *Pride*'s emergency evacuation procedure and managed to escape across the water by boat. Tilly is turning into an important source of information for me about Challener and what he might be up to. She knows things others don't. I think this potential mass slaughter was probably of his doing.'

'It does look that way, on the surface, at least.' Bose agreed. 'It certainly was one of his security team that

94

attempted to execute the slaughter. Unfortunately, he got away but his time will come. I only stumbled on it by chance.'

'Well, we do know that Challener wants to unsettle us because Tilly got wind from one of her sources. Apparently, unsettlement of the opposition is one of his tactics when in the role of predator. Maybe you and I should work closer together. What d'yer say?'

'Sounds good to me,' Bose replied.

'Well, let's drink to that. What'll you have? A whiskey?'

'Yes please. That would be fine.'

'Good, cos then I've got something to tell you. Eleanor!' His voice boomed out calling for the maid to come and fix their drinks. After she had done so, Hilliard bid Bose to sit with him at the table while Isabella sat on her favourite window seat.

'I need to lay my hands on the Ravine River Railroad Company's accounts. I bet they are inaccurate, fraudulent even, and if so I reckon that I could get the authorities to delay any further construction until a proper investigation has been carried out. The investigation could take weeks and Challener would probably have to lay off his workforce because he wouldn't be able to afford to pay them for sittin' around doin' nothin' while there is an embargo on the site.'

'Sounds good,' Bose responded encouragingly.

'The problem is it would mean breaking into railroad premises to steal them. Would you be prepared to do that? I would make sure that you are well compensated for such activity.'

'I'd be delighted to help,' Bose responded, pleased that the time for engagement with the enemy had now arrived. 'The Challeners owe your family and this is a chance to settle the score.'

'Good,' said Hilliard. 'Tilly has been able to get hold of the address and where exactly on the premises the accounts

are currently held. I will go and get the information for you.'
After he had left the room, Isabella spoke up.

'On the matter of that letter about my husband's supposed affair, you never gave me a definitive 'yes' or 'no'. Is that because you wondered if Tilly may have been having a relationship with Hilliard?'

'That's right,' Bose replied, 'but I think we can explain all that now. Don't you?'

'Yes, I think we can,' Isabella said with a knowing smile on her face.

'I expect you to come to me with solutions, not problems!' Burrell Challener shouted angrily at Carew Langdon. 'You're the second person this morning! First Senator Godefroy and now you! I can forgive the senator because he came to me with what I call a forgivable problem, one that is difficult to foresee occurring. But the problem you've given me could have been foreseen, even by a chimpanze!' Challener rose from his chair and started to pace the room. 'What the blazes made you want to try and blow up the *Pride of Probity*? You could have killed everyone aboard, innocent people! I can be hard-nosed if I have to be but only against people who deserve it, not innocent people, especially women and children.'

'We were after the killer of your brother, Mr Challener. Sorry, but you said we could try and find him and earn the reward,' Carew said apologetically, attempting to calm the situation down.

'Which particular person on that damned paddle steamer did you have in mind? Or do you think all of them killed him?' Challener demanded to know.

'Hilliard Rainecourt, Mr Challener, sir. It was he who killed your brother,' Langdon explained.

'And how do you know that?'

'My men are not professional bounty hunters but Bose Hendry is. So, we decided to follow him, let him lead us to the killer and then strike first. We saw Hendry on board the boat. Acting suspiciously, he was, especially near Rainecourt's suite.'

'So that makes him my brother's killer, does it?' Challener asked in disbelief.

'Hendry was after Rainecourt, trust me,' Landon answered. 'He was stalking him. Why else would he be doin' that?'

'How the hell do I know?' Burrell exclaimed, showing his frustration. 'But you haven't convinced me on the back of what you just said that Rainecourt's the man. It's weak, very weak, circumstantial evidence. An' even if he was the man, why risk killing everybody else? Why try and blow up the whole damned boat and everybody on it?'

'To make it look like an accident. A boiler room explosion. No one would be surprised at that. Most people would have been off the boat long before it caught fire. It was tied up. They could have got off anywhere along its portside.'

'Like the man you were after. Evidently, he got off it in double quick time in a damned rowing boat. So, you still wouldn't have got him. Fortunately, your plan was foiled and you can thank your adversary, Bose Hendry, for that. But your attempts have left me with a different problem; an unforgiveable one that you should have foreseen.'

'What's that?' Carew Langdon asked.

'Inadvertently, you and your men have changed the rules of engagement between the railroad and the Rainecourts,' Burrell said as he sat down in his chair again. He had admonished Langdon enough and had made him feel stupid and humiliated. Now he needed to appeal to his wayward employee's sense of reason again. 'You see, the interaction between us and the Rainecourts started off on a sound basis:

one of reason and logic. But your actions have raised the stakes considerably and the engagement will now turn into one based on emotion and attrition. The people of Probity will be thinking that we have tried to murder half of their population and that we are not reasonable people but feral animals. They are frontier people, so they will fight us to the death now because even if they ever doubted it, they now firmly believe that they are right and we are wrong. Any intelligent debate is over. Do you understand what I am saying?'

'Yes, Mr Challener, sir. So, so what next?' Carew Langdon asked sheepishly.

'First of all, you and your men are forbidden from entering Probity. You stay on the construction site unless I tell you otherwise. Failure to obey my orders and you'll all be sacked immediately and dismissed without pay. You see, Smokey was seen and recognized by Hendry. That news will spread like wildfire through the local community, quicker than Smokey envisaged that steamer catching fire. The people of Probity will be blamin' us and wondering where we're gonna strike next and what we're gonna do. We need to spread oil on troubled waters. I need to think some more on this before I decide what to do next, thanks to you.'

'Like I say, I'm sorry, Mr Challener, sir,' Langdon said, apologizing once again. Burrell Challener stared at him briefly, in silence. He took out a bottle of whiskey and two glasses from his drawer and after placing them on the top of the desk, proceeded to pour himself a glass. He then recorked the bottle.

'If you think you deserve a drink, then help yourself,' he said to Langdon. Burrell Challener watched in silence as his renegade head of security uncorked the bottle and poured himself a drink. This man needs more coaching than I gave him credit for if he is ever gonna realize his potential, Burrell thought to himself.

'OK, like I said earlier, I have another problem to solve. A forgivable one but it is no less urgent for that. I need you and your boys to do a little job for me.'

'Oh,' said Carew, feeling slightly more optimistic that the tide had turned and his dressing down was now over.

'It should be right up your street, so don't,' he stopped briefly for emphasis, 'screw up!'

'What's the job, Mr Challener?'

'I need to have the company accounts removed from our head office building and safely transported elsewhere. I can tell you exactly where they are, what room they are in, where the safe is and so on. The safe will be left open for you, so that bit is easy. It will need to be done tonight, preferably once it is dark.'

'We can do that for you, Mr Challener,' Carew Langdon said enthusiastically, unable to believe his luck.

'OK, but that's the easy bit. The harder bit is this. It needs to look like a break-in. I don't want the place all smashed up. Just a few bits of broken furniture, some broken windows that sort of thing.' he said. 'You and your boys can't afford to be seen even though it will be dark. Well, at least not recognized. You'll have to wear masks. There's something else,' he said thoughtfully. He stopped to take a swig of whiskey. His mind was on a roll. 'Right,' he said demonstrably. 'I think I've got it. If he doesn't have Bose Hendry on his back, Smokey's a good arsonist, yes?'

'Sure is,' Carew replied.

'His reputation is for starting wildfires but can he control one?'

'How do you mean?'

'Well,' Burrell began to explain. 'There's some outbuildings. Nothing much in them or not that we would want to keep. If they could be torched but the flames would need to be stopped from spreading to the main building. Some sort of fire break needed. I guess it probably depends on the wind direction. Listen, if Smokey can burn down the outbuildings and leave the main building intact, then all well and good but if he thinks there is any risk, then don't bother to try. Forget the idea.'

'I understand but why torch the outbuildings in the first place?' Carew Langdon asked.

'Because it will solve the problem you gave me earlier on. We will be able to accuse the people of Probity of undertaking a revenge attack, of burning down our property and risking other people's lives. It will be seen as a childish tit-for-tat exercise, where the final damage appears much worse than that inflicted on the *Pride of Probity* and means that the local community will have to concede some of the moral high ground they have recently won!

'But if Smokey screws up, tell him that I'll hand him on a plate to the people of Probity and they can do what they will with him because he'll no longer be in my employ!'

CHAPTER 14

'Looks like someone's beaten us to it,' Hilliard Rainecourt said in a disappointed tone, passing the latest edition of the *Probity Echo* across the table. Bose Hendry picked it up. They were breakfasting at Bose's favourite bar on the quayside, and sat outside in the early morning sun. He read the headlines. 'Break-in at Railroad HQ – Outbuildings destroyed by Fire'. The article went on to explain that the motives behind the burglary were unclear. It said that some furniture had been destroyed as if the thieves were searching for something and some documents were taken. The article speculated that they hadn't found exactly what they were looking for and may have set fire to the outbuildings out of frustration. It concluded by suggesting that the burglary and the fire could have been a revenge attack by angry people from Probity who were embittered by the recent attack on their iconic paddle steamer, which had been attributed to a railroad employee by many in the local community.

The final sentence was a quote from Burrell Challener, disclaiming any railroad involvement in the attack on the steamboat. 'My heart goes out to the people of Probity at this time and I want the perpetrator of this vicious attack on them to be brought to justice,' he exclaimed. 'Let's be clear, no employee of my railroad has ever been, or would be, authorized to attack innocent people in this way. We always try to work in harmony with the local communities on our routes in order to achieve the maximum benefit for all.'

'So, what do you make of that?' Hilliard asked as he poured them both some more black coffee. 'Do you think that's accurate reporting?'

'In as much as it reflects the views of the people the newspaper decided to interview,' Bose replied. 'The question is: do their views represent the truth? A distortion of the truth often makes for more interesting reading.'

'So, what do you think the truth is?' Hilliard Rainecourt asked.

'Well, certainly not all of the speculations as suggested by the *Echo*,' Bose replied. 'I can understand Challener pursuing a strategy of unsettlement if he is looking to oust a competitor, but blowing up a competitor is not implementing a strategy of unsettlement; it is implementing one of wanton destruction and potential mass murder. So, having thought more about it, I don't believe that Burrell Challener authorized the attack on the *Pride of Probity*, certainly not in terms of the intended outcome. Had it been successful, such an attack would quite rightly have totally destroyed his credibility with the local population and eventually would have put paid to his hopes of running a railroad in this area. But given that the attack was carried out by one of his employees, Challener is now faced with a damage limitation exercise of considerable proportions. Neither do I believe the so-called 'revenge attack' was carried out or authorized by the people of Probity. I think he probably carried out that attack himself.'

'As part of the damage limitation exercise?' Hilliard asked, becoming more intrigued.

'In part, yes but also to move the accounts and put them

in a safer place,' Bose replied. He thought for a moment and decided to keep his powder dry while he and Hilliard Rainecourt were still building trust in their personal relationship. 'I know and understand why you won't tell me who Tilly's informant is but I suspect it has to be someone in Burrell Challener's employ to be able to know the exact location of the company accounts. It also sounds to me like they are a double dealer and have pre-warned Challener of a likely break-in.'

Hilliard Rainecourt was temporarily left speechless. This man, my new partner, is very astute, he thought to himself. I might need to be a little bit careful about how much I tell him. 'Mmm,' he said thoughtfully. 'That's very clever analysis. The situation looks very different when you look at it like that, doesn't it?' he observed, regaining his composure. 'Same information but a totally different interpretation and an equally credible explanation! So, if you continued to put yourself in Mr Challener's shoes, where would you move the company accounts to for safe keeping?'

'Somewhere where they would be constantly under the noses of people who worked for you and were loyal to you,' Bose replied.

'Such as a railroad construction site?'

'Exactly that. The railroad construction site.'

'That's a pretty big place to look,' Hilliard remarked. 'Would you know where to begin looking?'

'Yes,' Bose replied. 'I think I do.'

CHAPTER 15

Bose Hendry figured that if Burrell Challener had stolen his own company's accounts the safest place to keep them on the construction site would be in the safe in Challener's private railcar at the end of the freshly laid track. Use of the car was a luxury and very few people would have been given access to it, unless Challener himself was present.

The inside of the car was divided into three sections: an office, a bedroom with en suite washing facilities and a lounge. The soft furnishings consisted mainly of leather, velvet and satin, with wooden furniture made of oak and top-grade mahogany wall panelling. Paintings were gilt framed, while items such as table lamps were finished in highly polished brass. The company books, Bose believed, would be stored in the office safe. Doubtless, they were a cleverly engineered set of documents, to which Burrell Challener and his directors would need regular access in order to ensure their whims and fancies were not running away with them.

The railcar's location was very close to the actual construction of the road itself during the daytime but at night was always kept at least half a mile away from the 'hell on wheels' tent city where the construction workers lived, slept and generally enjoyed themselves. Burrell Challener had quite correctly calculated that any of those who might fancy

sleeping or entertaining a whore in the luxury the car provided would find the journey too far to contemplate,
especially if laden down with a bellyful of booze.

For the timing of his robbery, Bose had chosen the hour
of the wolf, the hour at night when, according to his grand-
mother, people's energies levels were at their lowest, leaving
them vulnerable to the wolves that might come to their door.
He figured that during the hours of darkness, the railcar was
likely to be guarded by a member of Carew Langdon's team,
who would probably be experiencing his own personal hour
of the wolf just before the break of dawn after knocking
himself out with whiskey earlier on in the evening to relieve
the boredom of his work.

Finding the railcar in the dark was relatively easy. It was just
a case of heading for the lights of the 'hell on wheels' tent
town and then following the newly built road in the direction
of Probity. The only possible problem was being seen
approaching the town but Bose had already masked his face
below the eyes with his neckerchief and made sure that he
kept close to the shadows. Once safely beyond the tent town,
he dismounted and, having tied his horse to a tree, made the
final part of the journey on foot.

Approaching the railcar stealthily, he didn't notice anything untoward. Underneath it, however, he saw a sleeping
figure, wrapped up in a blanket and lying on a board that
straddled the gaps between the wooden ties. Bose picked up
a handful of grit and, crouching on his haunches with his
gun in his other hand, he tossed some of the grit at the sleeping man's face. The man stirred and as he rubbed the sleep
from his eyes, he banged his head on the underneath of the
carriage and swore loudly. Steadying himself, Bose threw the
remainder of the grit into the man's face, some of it landing
directly in his half-open eyes. The man swore again and

105

instinctively rolled onto his stomach, hoping that the force of gravity and the tears in his eyes would wash away the grit. As he rubbed his stinging eyes, he heard the ominous double click of a revolver hammer being pulled back. The man turned his head in the direction of the sound and saw the weapon was pointed at him.

The revolver's owner, who had been rude enough to wake him at such an ungodly hour, signalled to the man to crawl out slowly from under the car. He hesitated for a moment before obliging, wondering if he could grab his own gun on the way out, but thought better of it. The stranger didn't look like he was the sort of man interested in taking prisoners. As he crawled out from under the railcar, the masked man grabbed hold of him by the throat and flung him up against the side of the railcar.

'Huh! Well, if ain't Smokey, the Probity arsonist!' Bose mumbled from behind his mask.

'What do you want, mister? Who are yer?'

'All you need to know is that I am the masked man an' I want you to open the safe in this railcar.'

'I can pick the lock of the railcar but not the safe,' Smokey replied. Bose bundled him up the steps and pushed him toward the door of the car.

'Well, maybe this will help you,' Bose said, offering Smokey a stick of dynamite. From its short fuse, Smokey recognized it as the one he had tossed at Hendry on the *Pride of Probity*.

'I can't use that,' he said. 'The fuse wire's too short. We'd never get out of here alive.'

'I've thought of that,' Bose replied. 'Here!' He took a long piece of fuse wire from his pocket. 'Why don't you join that on to the short bit!'

Bose rode slowly in the early dawn light with the Ravine River Railroad Company's accounts in his saddle-bag, giving his horse a chance to recover. He pulled the mask down from his face, glad to breath in a lungful of fresh air again. Following the explosion, they had galloped for too long and Bose knew he needed to rest his horse. The exploding stick of dynamite had awoken many in the tent town and they were keen to investigate what had happened. What they found was a burnt-out railcar, an open, empty safe and Smokey at the bottom of the rear steps. In his haste to run from the car after he had lit the fuse, and still not fully awake, he had lost his footing, fallen down the steps and twisted his knee.

When Carew Langdon arrived, one of the last on the scene thanks to the previous night's excesses, he was at a complete loss to piece together what had actually happened. Some told him that they thought they had seen a lone rider flee the scene. If so, it was too late now to give chase but Carew reasoned that if someone else had been involved it would make it far easier to concoct a credible explanation for Burrell Challener of what might have happened. Unfortunately, Smokey would not be able to confirm the story because he was dead.

Isham Griffen awoke, as was his custom, at first light. He folded back the door of his tent, which was pitched on the edge of the woods, and walked around the back of the small shelter to where last night's fire was still smouldering. He boiled some water and made a fresh pot of black coffee. His assistant was still asleep in the adjacent tent. When the coffee had brewed, he poured himself a cup and, sitting down in his tent doorway, looked out across the open country in front to him. In the distance he could make out an unusual sight for that early in the morning, of a lone rider slowly crossing the range.

Isham went back inside and rummaged among his possessions for his Sharps buffalo rifle. With an effective firing range of over quarter of a mile, he reasoned that he should be able to pick off the rider from his tent, if he needed to. Looking through his pocket telescope to check if the rider might be hostile, he was surprised to see the head of Bose Hendry came into view. He realized that he would need to be quick. How this man whom he had come to see as his nemesis could be here in this position was an utter mystery but Isham decided it must be through some sort of divine providence. Realizing that such an opportunity was unlikely to occur again, he raised the rifle to his shoulder and began to wrap his index finger firmly around the trigger.

'Who you shooting at?' Isham's assistant asked, standing half-dressed outside the entrance to Isham's tent.

'That stranger out there,' Isham said. 'He looks to me as if he's been up to no good. I might need to put a warning shot over his head.'

'Did you hear the explosion, earlier on?' the assistant asked.

'Yes, I did,' Isham said, lowering the rifle as he looked at his assistant.

'Sounded like it came from the construction site. Maybe that rider knows something about it?'

'Yes, maybe you are right,' Isham said, raising the Sharps rifle to his shoulder once more.

It was by chance that Bose Hendry saw the early morning sunlight glint from a metal object close to the edge of the woods. He didn't know it was a Sharps buffalo rifle but his experience warned him that it was a gun of some sort and its holder was probably wanting to take a shot at him. He fired his revolver twice in the direction of the woods, turned his horse ninety degrees and disappeared at a gallop into the distance.

*

'I think you were right. He may well have known something,' Isham said to his assistant. He lowered the Sharps rifle to the ground, hoping that he wouldn't live to regret the missed opportunity.

CHAPTER 16

Isham Griffen unrolled the map on Burrell Challener's fold-away table. A coffee cup, an ashtray and two brass paper weights stopped the light breeze from rolling up the corners. Minor items that had been salvaged from the burnt-out railcar lay on the ground behind them.

'So where were you when you thought you saw Hendry?' Burrell asked.

'Here, exactly, Mr Challener,' Isham said, marking the map with a precise dot. 'This is where our tents are currently pitched.'

'And where did you see Hendry?' Burrell asked.

'On this scale map, it would be just here,' Isham said, indicating with his pencil, 'and this is where we presently are at the sidings by the head of the track.'

'So, not that far away from where you saw him, a couple of miles, say?'

'Two and three-quarters to be precise,' Isham said. 'Do you want us to do or say anything to him if we stumble across Hendry again?'

'No,' Burrell replied. 'We have no definite proof that it was him who stole the books and he'll know that, even though it certainly looks that way. If he comes on railroad land, of course, then Carew Langdon and his boys can deal

110

with the matter. And railroad land brings us to the real reason why I asked you here. What are your thoughts on the routing of the road: round or through Probity?'

'I have given this matter my utmost consideration,' Isham responded. 'If you'll allow me to do so I will talk you through the two alternative scenarios and the benefits and disbenefits of each.'

'Excellent,' said Burrell Challener. Feeling slightly lost without all the trappings and facilities of his railcar readily to hand, he pulled out a hip flask and offered Isham a drink. As Burrell anticipated, Isham, who was ready to launch into a discourse, dismissed the offer with a wave of his hand. Burrell put the flask to his own lips and sat back, ready to be enlightened.

'The two scenarios are . . .' Isham paused briefly to ensure that he had his employer's attention, 'to build the station at the back of the Rainecourts' property, thus bringing the road as close as possible to the village of Probity. Yards and depots would thus be built on the side of the track furthest away from Probity. Now, you will have noticed that I have referred to Probity in this option – scenario one – as a village. I use this noun as a relative term in this context and will come back to it again later. This is the cheapest solution in terms of cost per mile but only marginally so at two decimal places with building and land development opportunities limited to one side of the track only. That is unless one were to raze the existing village to the ground and redevelop the site. There is no difference in the technical considerations regarding track laying between this scenario and scenario two.'

'Got it,' said Burrell, ever quick to assimilate information. 'Go on,' he urged.

'Scenario two allows for the track to pass Probity almost three miles away from the current village site. This will maximise the ability to secure land either side of the tracks at the special discount rate offered by the state in the charter. The addition of a railroad to the current waterway will make this area a transport hub and as such land prices should rise rapidly and by significant multiples. Keeping the track a few miles away from Probity as it currently stands will enable a town to be developed on this cheap land. The current village of Probity will eventually become the old quarter of this town. With an attractive 'old town' and more of a 'resort'-style waterfront, Probity could attract a luxury tourist trade as part of its portfolio of commercial interests.' Isham stopped and looked at Challener firmly in the eye, which Burrell had learned normally indicated that his young, genius engineer had completed his monologue.

'That's it?' he asked, seeking reassurance.

'Yes, sir,' Isham said.

'Do you as an engineer have a preference and if so what is it?'

'That's an interesting question, if I may be so bold, sir. As an engineer, I have no preference. Technically it's as easy to build the track for scenario one as it is for scenario two. There are no real variations in grade or curvature, to speak of. Scenario two marginally increases the price per mile as the road will take a wider sweep around Probity. The overall price also increases but by an insignificant amount relative to the overall construction cost of the completed road. I am less of an expert in such matters as town planning but the potential commercial value of pursuing scenario two cannot be ruled out without due consideration to its merits, which would outweigh, financially at least, any other factors that may be taken into account.'

'I see,' said Burrell, having already made up his mind. 'Well, thank you very much for your thoughts. I will need to reflect on this but will come back to you tomorrow,' he said, keen to let Isham know that the authority to make such a decision rested with him alone.

*

Hilliard Rainecourt welcomed his accountant to his private suite on board the *Pride of Probity* and offered him a glass of whiskey. As Hilliard poured their drinks, his accountant removed the Ravine River Railroad Company books from his leather briefcase and spread them out on Hilliard's desk. He also took out a two-page summary of his findings, which he started to browse through.

'Your good health,' Hilliard said, offering his guest a glass of the finest whiskey.

'Thanks, yours too,' the accountant said. There was a clink of crystal as they touched glasses in a toast to their longevity.

'So, what did you make of Challener's books?' Hilliard asked.

'Well, I suspect his financial people are busy making up another set as we speak. It shouldn't be too difficult if it's based on the same scanty set of records as these probably are. Also, as a general point, the company's bankers must have seen these but I would be concerned and worried if they have issued bonds or loans to the company on the back of this information. There are a number of clear discrepancies with the published company accounts as well, but that is not surprising because, alas, many railroads' published accounts are works of fiction based on even scantier information than their management accounts, which in themselves are insufficient to provide good management and control of the business. They are my main general comments, which are supported by more specific observations.'

'Go on,' said Hilliard enthusiastically, his mind already starting to conjure up ways in which he might be able to leverage such damaging information.

'The problem is that one doesn't know if many of the entries can be taken at face value. On one hand, the books are probably accurate when they show in the notes that Senator Godefroy and all his fellow directors at the company's bankers, who also sit on the board of Challener's railroad company, have been given free travel passes for several years now. This is not the sort of information that one would normally disclose as it raises other issues. The directors' salaries are very high for a company struggling to make a profit, implying in the case of the bank directors that they have been swollen by additional personal payments. A free travel pass is often just a euphemism for throwing the bankers a personal bung if they continue to award dodgy loans to the company and issue bonds on the company's behalf, which at the outset they know the company is going to have to borrow or misrepresent in the accounts, in order to pay the interest.'

'So, is there evidence of that?' Hilliard asked.

'Indirectly, there is,' his accountant answered. 'According to these books, the amount that has supposedly been spent on maintenance and repairs is very high. But as everybody knows who rides the Ravine River Railroad, the track is badly worn in places and the trains themselves subject to frequent breakdown. This would not be the case if the money that is booked here to maintenance and repairs was actually spent on the same. I suspect it has been used to finance new construction and pay loan interest and dividends due on existing bonds. The whole thing is a merry-go-round.'

'But it will all implode, won't it?' Hilliard asked, surprised at the total lack of integrity displayed by his new competitor.

'Of course it will!' his accountant agreed. 'It is not sustainable to keep afloat just by borrowing alone and hoping that one day your operating income will increase sufficiently to cover not only your operating costs but fixed ones as well, such as servicing existing borrowings. There are two things that will kill off the railroads: one is overcapacity, which we are already seeing the effects of. The other will be a collapse in the European bond markets for railroad bonds because bondholders find more lucrative and secure places to invest their money. Then the magic money roundabout will stop spinning!'

'Leading to receivership?' Hilliard prompted.

'Exactly,' the accountant agreed. 'Then the auditors will discover the fraudulent nature of the books but until that day, when people will get badly burnt, everyone thinks everything is OK.'

'So, it is to our advantage that we know different, then?' Hilliard commented. 'Is Challener's company far away from collapse?'

'It is to our advantage, but as I said earlier, the problem with sets of books like these is that some parts of them will invariably be accurate, or at least be a reasonable reflection of what is actually going on. Other parts will not be. The trouble is, looking at them without access to the original bills, invoices and income receipts, which certainly won't exist in their entirety, we don't know which bits are which. The financial director will, no doubt, have a fair idea but he will be the only person. So, bearing in mind that serious caveat, my guess is that Burrell Challener could be only a pay day or two away from being unable to pay the wage bill!'

'And it will be the construction workers who won't get paid because their current costs aren't generating any income,' Hilliard observed with satisfaction.

'That's exactly right,' his accountant agreed.

Later that evening, Bose was invited to join Hilliard Rainecourt as his personal guest in his private suite on the *Pride of Probity*. Bose observed the same opulence that he had seen, albeit in the dark, inside Burrell Challener's personal railcar recently, on the night that, with the help of the now sadly departed Smokey, he had removed the books of the Ravine River Railroad Company from their supposed hiding place. He wasn't that surprised about the wealth that permitted such luxuries; after all he was mixing in elite circles – the world of the powerbrokers and the driven, those who could bypass society's system of checks and balances if the infrastructure that they controlled was at risk of imploding and, like it or not, the influencers and shapers of other people's lives.

'We've analysed the books,' said Hilliard. 'They don't look good, well at least not for Burrell Challener, although their dubious content is potentially a good omen for us. I need you to do a job for me. I think we know each other well enough now to trust each other, wouldn't you agree?' Bose nodded. 'The source of some of the inside information I have about Challener and his business comes from Senator Godefroy. He is not a willing participant in this endeavour, mind you. For a man who is held in high public esteem as a senator, bank director and upstanding citizen, he has an unfortunate Achilles heel: at times, he has been a man of serious lapsed morals. I know this through Tilly, an ex-sporting lady.

'Personally, I am not an advocate of blackmail and I had to wrestle with my conscience before selling the idea to Tilly and persuading her to participate in my plan. But it was a case of needs must and given the information we now have, the means have justified the ends. The time has come, however, for Tilly to cease her participation in this seedy scheme. Indeed, it is time for this seedy little scheme to stop. And that is where you come in. I need you to explain this to Senator Worth Godefroy. I suspect he will be secretly delighted but such delight comes at a price, so I want you to put one last proposal to him.'

Senator Godefroy took out his pocket watch, checked the time and let out a frustrated sigh. 'That damned woman's late,' he muttered to himself. As he looked nervously around the graveyard, he was startled by a sudden movement behind him.

'She ain't late, senator. She ain't comin', today you got me, instead!'

'Hendry!' Senator Godefroy exclaimed. 'It's you. You are in league with that woman, Tilly, aren't you? Ah, I get it now, you're both working for Rainecourt, aren't you?'

'You ask too many questions, Senator. Look, I work for no one. I'm a free agent. Always have been. Unlike you, up to your neck in shady deals. You are like one of those marionette puppets in danger of being strangled by your own strings because everyone else is pullin' them! But fear not. I've come to help you wipe the slate clean and rid yourself of your puppet masters so that you can start again as a free man.'

'Huh, smart talk, Hendry. So, who would you suggest my puppet masters are if it is not you and that Tilly woman?' the senator demanded to know.

'Hmm,' said Bose Hendry thoughtfully as he casually sat down on a tombstone. 'I think you probably have three. Let me see. I would suggest Burrell Challener for one. I suspect that he could be quite a demanding man. Then, of course, there are your fellow directors at the bank. I suspect none of them would want to jump off the financial gravy train soon even it was prudent to do so. Then there is the third group, who I am here representing today. They are a small group of concerned customers of your bank.

'Now, Senator. If you were to put those three groups in an order, starting with the ones who are likely to give you the most grief, what would that order be?'

'Burrell Challener would be at the top of my list without any doubt,' the senator said. 'Always wants the impossible and wants it done by yesterday. Then, my fellow directors at the bank. They are OK though, not much of a problem. We do disagree sometimes but that is healthy for managers of a business to do that.'

'And, last, the customers, then?' said Bose Hendry.

'Yes, they are never any problem. Customers trust the custodians of a good bank and we are a good bank,' Godefroy said with pride.

'That's interesting,' Hendry commented, 'because as an outside observer I would have thought your list would be in totally the reverse order.' Senator Godefroy looked at Hendry full of surprise and curiosity. 'You see, personally, I wouldn't see Burrell Challener as much of a problem. The man is, as you are no doubt aware, a liar and a cheat and I don't have much time for those sorts of people. If they start getting' on my nerves, then I just get 'em out of my life. But that's the difference between you and me. I don't allow people like that to use me but you do. You think you are very important to him but he only wants you when it suits him. For example, you probably didn't know about the railroad's accounts being stolen.'

'Of course I did,' the senator interjected. 'It was all over the newspaper!'

'Ah yes the scam robbery, where Challener stole his own accounts so that he could blame it on the people of Probity. You knew about that, I'm sure!'

'Yes, I did,' said the senator, hanging his head in shame.

'I bet Challener didn't tell you that since then the accounts have been stolen for real. Taken in the middle of the night from the safe in his personal railcar. Big explosion, left his railcar totally burnt out, beyond repair.'

'What!' the senator exclaimed. 'I, I'd heard about the railcar being badly damaged. I thought that it was a group of drunken workers. In fact, I asked Burrell if that was who damaged his car and he certainly didn't deny it! So, someone blew the safe open to get the books!'

'It would seem that way,' Bose agreed quietly.

'So, how do you know all this?' Worth Godefroy, demanded. 'If those books fall into the wrong hands, it could be very serious, you know?'

'I know,' Hendry agreed. 'And I suspect Burrell Challener does as well, which is why he has hushed up the details of the real robbery. Set too many hares running.'

'I don't believe you,' Senator Godefroy suddenly interjected. 'It's not true. You're making this up! I think you're up to something!'

'That's a matter of personal opinion,' Bose Hendry said, 'but I know it's true that the books were stolen from the safe in the railcar, 'cos I stole them!' Speechless, the senator's jaw dropped open and his face turned ashen. 'Which brings me to why I would put your small group of concerned customers at the top of the list for being able to cause you the most grief,' Bose continued. 'You see, they are not very happy with the content of those books and indeed, the lack of it. As a result, they have lost confidence in the directors of the bank to manage their savings and investments. They are concerned that you and your colleagues, who as the Ravine River Railroad Company's bankers, must know the dire state of their client's financial position but appear content to risk their other clients' hard-earnt savings on yet another 'last' spin of the magic money roundabout, issuing another 'last' set of loans, and another 'last' new bond issue. All in anticipation of a bumper payday when the railroad's sister company, which speculates in land and property, spews out profits from the increased land and property values from the redevelopment of Probity. Now these disgruntled customers probably wouldn't feel so bad if they sat on the boards of all three companies involved in this incestuous arrangement, but they don't and are never likely to be invited to.'

'They may be disgruntled but there is little they can do about it,' Senator Godefroy exclaimed. 'If there are any accounting irregularities as you suggest, the bank would obviously put them right and update any policies and procedures that needed amending to ensure a continuation of good working practices. I'm afraid you overstate the drama of the situation.'

'Drama is an appropriate way to describe it,' Bose commented. 'Perhaps, that's how those disgruntled customers see it. Like a drama – a tragedy even: an uncontrollable forest fire burning all their money. And Senator Godefroy, you know what spreads faster than an out of control forest fire?'

'No, but I suspect you are going to tell me,' the senator said with frustration.

'A run, on a bank. Once it starts, word travels like wild fire and it is very difficult to stop. You can control a fire by starving it of oxygen but you can't control a run on a bank if you have already starved it of trust. Did you know that? That's why I would put the disgruntled customers at the top of the grief list. Then, I would put your fellow bank directors second. They won't like being dictated to from outside their circle. It's not how the elite operate but once they get over that I am sure that they will see sense. And then Burrell Challener will end up bottom of the grief list and be no trouble at all. You see, you can't run a railroad if you've been starved of debt because someone's stopped the loan roundabout from going around.'

The senator realized that he couldn't win. He looked crestfallen. He sat down on the tombstone and silently looked at the ground. This certainly didn't feel like a good situation to be in but Hendry had to offer him something, if he wanted any leverage himself. Bose Hendry did not seem like the sort of man who would totally crush another man's spirit just for the hell of it. In that respect, he was no Burrell

Challener, in spite of clearly being a shrewd operator.

'What do you want, Hendry and what's in it for me?'

'Smart thinking, senator. Smart thinking,' Bose said encouragingly. 'This group of disgruntled customers whom I represent wants Burrell Challener's railroad activities curtailed. They are frightened that he is gonna bring the bank down. They believe, from his own accounts by the way, not the published ones, that he is overstretched and basically gambling with other people's money.'

'And how, prey do you think that I can bring that about and do it unscathed?'

'Simple,' Bose replied. 'I understand that you can be a persuasive man when it comes to business. I want you to persuade your fellow directors on the bank's board not to undertake any more bond issues and not to make any more unsecured or poorly secured loans to Challener until the outstanding ones are paid back in full.'

'But that will break him!' Worth Godefroy exclaimed.

'Maybe,' Bose acknowledged, 'but the alternative would be a run on the bank, which could break it, the source of most of your income. And I wouldn't fear reprisals from Challener either. He is not a vindictive person and will realize that he has nothing to gain from taking his disappointment out on you. He'll be away on to his next project.'

'You've only partially answered my question about what's in it for me?' Godefroy pointed out.

'So, I have,' Bose agreed. 'Pardon me. Let's see what's in it for you, then. Well, as I have already explained, the bank keeps its reputation, you keep it as a source of income, but probably what you are wanting me to spell out is that your personal reputation will not only remain intact but will probably be enhanced through what will be seen as an act of good citizenship. Tilly, who is the only one who knows about your secrets, will not darken your door again and what happened in the past will stay in the past. If you do as the people I represent ask, the Ravine Railroad Company's missing books will be returned to you as the company's official bankers. Do with them what you will. You personally and your bank have nothing to lose, only everything to gain, if we have a deal.'

'We have a deal,' Senator Godefroy said as he shook Bose Hendry's hand.

CHAPTER 17

'Excuse me ma'am,' said Eleanor as she walked into the drawing room and shut the door behind her. 'You have a visitor in the hall. He is rather insistent that he wants to see you. It's Mr Isham Griffen.' Isabella felt a tightness in her stomach and took a deep breath to calm herself.

'You can show him in, Eleanor. Please bring us some tea after a few minutes and then stay on hand, near the hallway. When I feel it is time for him to go, I will ring for you on the pretext of ordering more refreshment. Come in and remind me that my next appointment is due.' She had almost put this man out of her mind and was wary of being in his company after she and Bose had concluded that he could be the murderer of Seth Challener.

'Mrs Rainecourt, I am delighted to see you again,' Isham Griffen said, standing in the doorway, his manners preventing him from proceeding any further, unless invited.

'It is a pleasure to see you too, Mr Griffen.' She lied convincingly as the rules of civility demanded a lady should do. 'Please, come in.' She showed him across to the window seat on the other side of the room but chose to sit down herself at the table between the window seat and the drawing room door.

'I must apologize for turning up uninvited,' he said, 'but I was passing and wanted to share some good news with you.'

'Oh, I am fond of good news,' Isabella said smiling. 'Pray tell me, what is yours?'

'I learnt this morning that Mr Challener has accepted my recommendation as regards the location of the railroad track at Probity.'

'Go on,' she urged.

'Well, he has agreed that the track should not pass through Probity itself but be laid a few miles outside of town where the station and a railyard will be established. Also, he doesn't want to redevelop Probity itself. He sees this as being the picturesque 'old quarter' of a newer, much bigger town. Probity, as we know it today, will become an artist and tourist quarter. Isn't that good news? All the hard work you have put into planning and designing this oasis will not be wasted.'

'Yes, indeed,' Isabella said. 'Thank you for the news and your appreciation.' Isham felt himself melt under the warmth of her smile and her sincere recognition of his achievement. Although he recalled feeling like this when he had first met her, Isham subsequently rationalized correctly that in her absence such fancy would fade. Yet the strong feeling of physical attraction he was feeling towards her at this moment was proving that rationale undeniably wrong.

On a non-physical, non-emotional level, however, Isham had often thought how he and Isabella Rainecourt might make the perfect intellectual pairing and in moments of extreme boredom had conjured up scenarios where her husband, Hilliard, and male friend Bose Hendry might no longer figure in her life and leave the way clear for them to fulfil their brilliance together. Those dark scenarios were starting to flare up in his mind again, as if to test his true feelings for Isabella. He tried desperately to suppress them so this most gracious of hostesses would not think that he had become distracted.

Fortunately, such embarrassment was prevented by the arrival of Eleanor with their refreshment. By the time she had poured the tea and passed the milk jug and sugar bowl around, followed by a plate of biscuits, Isham was back in control of his demeanour. However, those dark thoughts that he had managed to suppress had left a slight stain on his topic of conversation.

'Unfortunately, not everything is such good news, Mrs Rainecourt,' he said quietly, turning the conversation in a different direction.

'Oh,' Isabella said with a hint of concern in her voice as she wondered where this might be leading. Isham got up from the window seat and came and joined her at the table.

'As you are probably aware, there is a lot of trouble afoot. Many dealings of an underhand nature are taking place. Some people who others considered to be loyal have been found wanting and guilty of betrayal. I know of these things through my work but I am sorry, I have said too much, probably because I know too much.'

'I don't understand, Mr Griffen. Please explain yourself,' Isabella said, now hoping to clear the air by having the conversation she hadn't wanted to have. Isham took her request literally, as the green light to share with her some of the darker things that were on his mind, which he wouldn't have done if he hadn't fallen again under Isabella's spell.

'Well,' he said hesitatingly. 'You see, I really fear for your safety in such times. It is very difficult to know who to trust here anymore, including those who you hold close.'

'I thank you for your concerns about my personal welfare, Mr Griffen but please be more specific about the generalities of which you speak,' Isabella asked.

'It is difficult because I don't want to hurt your feelings but take for example your friend, Bose Hendry. Trouble seems to follow him around. Following the incident on the

Pride of Probity, Mr Hendry emerged as a hero but since then his status has fallen dramatically. Some say he is responsible for the wanton destruction of Mr Challener's personal railcar and also the death of one of his employees. What kind of civilised society are we living in if one moment someone is regarded as a hero and the next moment a murderer? How do we know in whom, we can place our trust and in whom, we can't?'

'I agree that we are living through troubled times, Mr Griffen,' Isabella conceded, 'but rumours abound under such circumstances and the truth often remains hidden. We have to keep the faith until it emerges and proves us either right or wrong.' Isham Griffen was disappointed by Isabella's reaction. She clearly hadn't fully grasped his point, which was unusual because most people invariably accepted his logic without question.

'Let me explain myself clearer,' he said composing himself. 'This example might be difficult for both of us but I think it will make my point more accessible for you. When I first met you, I brought you a sealed letter, the content of which, I told you I was unaware. I lied about that because I didn't know you and it was a delicate matter for a stranger to tell another stranger about their spouse.'

'About my husband's supposed affair?' Isabella exclaimed, trying to conceal the shock in her voice. Isham noticed her looking hesitantly at the hand bell on the table, used to call the maid. Needing to have her full attention, he removed this source of distraction to his end of the table where she was unable to reach it. 'So, how do you know the content of it? It wasn't written by you. It was written by Seth Challener,' she said in an icy tone.

'Because he told me what was in it. I was with him in that stagecoach, the night that he died,' Isham said in a matter of fact way.

'But he was murdered, strangled!' Isabella gasped.

'That is popular conjecture, I agree,' said Isham. 'But that's not what actually happened. I know, I was there. This is precisely my point. How do we know who we can trust around here, anymore? Innocent people can be maligned and punished while the guilty get away completely free.'

'So, what actually did happen to Seth Challener and why did he think my husband was having an affair? I need to know the truth, Mr Griffen!'

'Of course, you do, Mrs Rainecourt and I shall tell you and dispel any fearful thoughts you might be having. I met Seth Challener in the grand saloon of the *Pride of Probity* earlier on that fateful evening. I didn't know who he was. As far as I was concerned he was just another card player who I thought, as I play very scientifically, I could win a lot of money from. But I failed to keep my concentration at one point and was proved to be wrong; he thrashed me but he had cheated. Unfortunately, I was unable to prove it as he smartly destroyed the evidence but we both knew what had really happened. I was absolutely fuming but still had the presence of mind to recall that he had mentioned earlier that he was staying at the Probity Grand Hotel. He would have had to catch the stage, which hadn't left yet, so I thought I might be able to meet with him there.

'My reasoning was correct and we ended up on board the same stage, with no other passengers. As the coach started its winding journey up the cliff face, we started fighting. I got the better of Challener and grabbed his satchel. The letter addressed to you was in there. He told me of the contents and offered me the letter if I left him alone. He reasoned that eventually you might be prepared to pay dearly for the next instalment of information.'

'Which was?' Isabella said sharply.

'Oh that, your husband's mistress was an ex-whore called

Tilly. Seth Challener figured that you would pay handsomely to keep that information quiet rather than have the good name of the Rainecourt family sullied.'

'And did you deliver the letter to me so that I would then pay you handsomely instead?'

'No,' Isham replied. 'I used it purely as a chance opportunity to meet you. I had heard that you were a fine woman, one of virtue and honour and I must say, you live up to your reputation and are an exceptional lady. I also knew our paths would cross due to the location of the railroad. I thought we might work well together to solve this social issue. I have to say Mrs Rainecourt, meeting you has certainly not disappointed me and you have exceeded my expectations.' Isabella bowed her head in acknowledgement of the frank but unusual expression of flattery. 'Besides, even if Seth Challener's accusation regarding your husband was true, it was no business of mine and not something I was interested in or wished to become involved with.'

'So, how exactly did Mr Seth Challener die, Mr Griffen? Do you know?' Isabella asked coldly, challenging Isham Griffen to tell the truth.

'Yes, I do and I will tell you,' Isham responded calmly. 'I pocketed the letter addressed to you and continued to rummage through his bag for my money but to no avail. So, I then started going through his pockets. We began fighting again. We fell to the floor and as the stage rounded a bend, the door flew open and Challener started falling out. I tried to save him and grabbed hold of his jacket but it was poor quality and came off in my hands. Challener started to slide down the cliff face on his back but as he did so, his satchel became ensnared on a dead tree root. With its shoulder strap caught under his chin, his body weight caused the buckle to press sharply into his throat.

'As the stagecoach slowed for the next bend, I jumped out

128

and climbed down the slope, to try and free him. The weight of his body pulling on the dead tree root, however, caused the nodule from which he was suspended, to break. He went into free fall, bouncing off the cliff face on his descent and onto the rocks below, before finally ending up in the river.'

Isabella said nothing at first as her mind absorbed Isham Griffen's account of Seth Challener's death. Sensationalists would have described it as incredible but her rational, thinking mind could see that it was plausible; just a different interpretation of the facts as people thought they knew them. It was the plausibility of that story that started to give Isabella a feeling of relief. Perhaps she could trust Isham Griffen after all. Finally, she spoke.

'So, did Seth Challener have your money?' Isabella asked.

'Yes,' Griffen replied. 'I found it afterwards, tucked away in the lining of his jacket. I had the right man.'

'Perhaps, you should tell the authorities your account of what happened?' she said.

'There's little point. I am not an official suspect and with the way things are around here at the moment, how could I trust the justice system, with everybody pointing the finger at everybody else?'

'Have you told anyone else what you just told me?' Isabella asked anxiously.

'No. Why should I?'

'Because you told me?'

'I told you because I wanted there to be trust between us. That's why I told you something, in good faith about me, which could leave me vulnerable, in order to build that trust,' Isham explained.

'I understand,' Isabella said, 'and I thank you for it,' she said, feeling nervous again. She knew she needed to get rid of this creepy man. 'Pass me the bell, please and I will ring for some more tea,' she said.

'I will only be gone a few days, ma'am, but I am afraid my mother is very ill.'

'That's not a problem, Eleanor,' Isabella said, trying to reassure her loyal maid. 'Take as long as you need to. I do hope your dear mother makes a full recovery.'

'Is there anything you want doing, before I leave?' Eleanor asked.

'Just leave this note for Bose with the purser on board the *Probity*. In it, I explain my latest concerns about Mr Griffen.'

'Yes, of course, ma'am and remember: when Mr Rainecourt's out of the house make sure all the external doors and windows are secure and at night lock yourself in your bedroom.'

'I will, Eleanor. Thank you,' Isabella replied.

CHAPTER 18

'So, Carew, what's the mood of the workers in your opinion?' Burrell Challener asked. He could see that his head of security was distracted by his surroundings. Burrell was not surprised. His new personal railcar was as well appointed as the one that had been destroyed. The car had been built to the personal specification of the chairman of a competitor railroad, which had recently gone into receivership and as such had become surplus to requirements. Challener hadn't bought it at a fire sale but even so had managed to procure it at a very reasonable price. It wasn't decorated exactly to his personal taste but that didn't matter because it met his key criterion, of being a visual display of sheer opulence.

'The men are, how can I put it, not totally sure of what is going on. There is an underlying air of hostility towards the railroad company. They feel that they might be being taken for a ride but they are not too sure why,' Carew explained. 'They don't understand, for example, why the company's bankers are refusing to advance any more loan money when up to now they have fully supported the investment in this new road.'

'It's like this,' Burrell interjected. 'Have you ever over-spent and found that you can't really afford to buy that extra bottle of whiskey you were so looking forward to? And then a month later you find yourself flush and have more money in your pocket than you could possibly drink away?'

'Yes, I have,' said Carew Langdon hesitantly, wondering what point the boss was trying to make.

'Well the bank has done the same thing. They've over-spent a bit and are now having to rein it in. It'll pass.'

'You certain about that, Mr Challener?'

'Yes, of course I am,' said Burrell, always able to muster sufficient confidence, whatever the crisis. 'If you manage your affairs with a degree of caution, as I do, the bad times pass and you can look forward to a rosy future again. I have given the men signs of my confidence, if they took the trouble to reflect on what I have done for them. Take this railcar, for example. Tomorrow, it will be back in its rightful place at the head of the road. Do you think I would have bought another car if I wasn't confident about the future?'

'I think some of the men might see it as an extravagance and the money spent on it could have been used to pay the men their wages in full, in cash,' Langdon commented.

'With all due respect, that is the thinking of the small man. Big man's thinking is looking for those signs that the future is gonna be OK and realizing that the purchase of this car is an indicator of a prosperous future. Listen, I could have paid the men just half of their wages due in cash and told them that as times are bad, they'll just have to make do. I could have even reduced their wages and told them that that is the new going rate for the job. But I haven't done that, have I, Carew?'

'No, Mr Challener.'

'So, what have I done?'

'You paid half their wages in cash and the other half in bonds, which are not as readily exchangeable as cash.'

'Yes, I have given the workers unsold bonds, at face value, from the last company issue. In easier times we would have sold all of those on the markets to raise capital. Now, the wise among the men will realize that a fixed rate of interest is payable, periodically, on those bonds. That is extra money over and above whatever the bond's value might be in the marketplace. In other words, it is a bonus. You see, soon, those bonds will be able to be sold, for a profit. Their value will increase as the bad times pass. Be worth more than the wages, if I had paid the men in cash.'

'But that's the problem, Mr Challener. A black market has already started on the construction site and some men are selling their bonds at less than face value to try and make up for the shortfall in their wages. It's starting to get nasty and divisive, pitting different groups of workers against each other.'

'Well, as part of your role as head of security, it's your job to keep the peace among the workers. Tell them that if any of them cause trouble you have my permission to throw them off the site.'

'I think the problem is potentially bigger and more complicated than that, Mr Challener.' Burrell raised his hand to indicate to Langdon to stop speaking while he lit himself a cigar. He took his time, watching the flame on the match flare up as he dragged on the cigar and then die down. The display was not intended to be one of ostentation but to allow Burrell to get a grip on his temper before it exploded. Why did Langdon always come to him with problems and never solutions?'

'In what way?' Challener asked.

'Some men understand all that buying and selling bonds stuff but others don't. Like I say, many have sold their bonds to their fellow workers in order to raise some badly needed cash in hand but at far too cheap a price, and as a consequence they are not going to make it through to next pay day.' Carew paused, hoping that he was going to be offered a cigar. When he saw that no such offer was forthcoming, he realized that he was going to have to play hard ball. Both men were starting to become irritated with each other.

'So, what do they expect me to do about it?' Burrell asked with indignation.

'Well, those who have bought bonds from their colleagues and know what they are doing think you should buy their holding back at face value or market rate, whichever is the higher.'

'So, they effectively get a bonus!' Burrell exclaimed. 'And what about those who don't know what they are doing and have sold their bonds at rock bottom prices?'

'They just wanna be paid the other fifty per cent of their wages, in cash.'

'Or else?'

'Or else they're gonna go on strike. They probably represent a third of the workforce. The problem is that they are not all unskilled workers who could easily be replaced. Some of them are highly skilled.'

'So, what do you think I should do?' Burrell demanded to know, fearful that his head of security was presenting each piece of this bad news to him as if he was not only about to checkmate his employer but was also enjoying the process of doing so. Carew paused to take out a plug of tobacco and roll himself a smoke. He needed to play his next moves carefully.

'Well, one option is to let the men strike. That could become a war of attrition and if so would be an additional cost in terms of eventually reaching some sort of a settlement. If it were me, I would buy back any bonds that the men wished to sell, and they won't all wanna sell them, at face value to make good the shortfall in their cash wages,' Carew said.

'Mmm,' Burrell responded thoughtfully. 'Under the circumstances, a half-intelligent suggestion coming from you.

The only problem is, if the bank won't lend us any more funds, where do I get the money from?'

'Sell other assets. Like this railcar for example, rather than risk it being torched. Depends on what other assets there are to sell, of course, and the trade-off between what they earn the company today compared with what the new railroad will earn,' Carew said calmly and confidently. It was this last piece of advice and its delivery that stuck in Burrell's craw. He hadn't been expecting an insightful or intelligent answer.

'Tell me, Langdon. Don't you see it as your job to stop this railcar from being torched?'

'Under normal circumstances, yes but not when the construction workers could riot. With Smokey gone we are a man down and would not be able to hold a united, militant front. The best we could do is maybe turn some of the divided factions among the workers against each other but that's a different skill,' Carew emphasized. 'Besides, that's not what we are being paid to do.'

'And how much do you think you should be paid to do that?' Burrell asked, feeling his wrath rising.

'At least double what we get now,' Carew said calmly, playing his final move. Burrell slammed his fist down on the table.

'Checkmate, Langdon! You and your men are fired!' he exclaimed angrily.

CHAPTER 19

In order to try and find Isham Griffen, Bose decided the best place to start his search was at the 'hell on wheels' town that followed the construction of the new railroad as it snaked its way across the range. In spite of its reputation for enabling the lowest forms of human indulgence, the gratuitous nature of the tent town and many of its inhabitants actually provided good cover for making discreet enquiries. Many were either too wasted or just plain disinterested in the underlying political nature of such enquiries to recall later who might have asked them what about who. Most people wanted to be helpful and answer any seemingly innocent question, honestly, almost out of an act of citizenship.

In spite of such generosity from the locals, Bose learnt very little about the whereabouts of Isham Griffen. Most people he spoke to had heard of the name but very few claimed that they would have recognized the surveyor even if he crossed their path. Although fundamental to the design of the writhing metal snake, most workers took their daily instructions from lesser mortals in the hierarchy, rather than the feted, construction engineer, Isham Griffen. The most common information that Bose received on his whereabouts suggested that Griffen and his assistant camped well away from the tent town in a wooded area some distance ahead of where the track currently ended. A few, however, said that they had actually seen Griffen earlier that morning on the other side of the town, inspecting track that had already been built. The most interesting information Bose received was the speculation and rumours that were doing the rounds about the workers' immediate futures.

'I hear Challener is comin' to pay us our proper wages,' said the bearded man who was sat at a wooden table, near the door of a large tent which housed a bar. 'I hear that his arrival is imminent.'

'You stopped workin' 'til then, have yer?' his colleague with the barrel chest asked.

'Too damned right, I have,' replied the man with the beard, as he poured himself another glass of whiskey. 'Why should I work when I can afford not to? I sold my bonds for more than face value when there was that spike in demand the other day and some folk thought if they bought them then they were gonna get rich quick.'

'I still got mine,' said the man with the barrel chest. 'Maybe I should have done the same but I'm hangin' onto mine now. Rumour yesterday goin' round the Pig's Head café that Challener's gonna buy them back for just face value.'

'The question is,' said a man with a large beer gut who waddled into the tent to take refuge from the midday sun, 'will Challener buy back all those from people who have increased their holdings because they have bought extra from other people? Phew, it's hot out there!'

'It ain't much better in here,' the bearded man was quick to point out. Bose Hendry agreed with the man's observation. Although people inside the tent were in the shade, there was no breeze and the air hung hot, humid and heavy. However, the conversation was interesting so Bose ordered

137

himself another beer. It was more refreshing than drinking whiskey.

'What makes you think he won't?' the man with the barrel chest asked.

'Dunno,' Beer Gut replied, 'but I got talkin' to Carew Langdon and some of his boys last night an' it got me thinkin' about what Challener might actually do.'

'I thought Langdon had been sacked?' the bearded man said.

'He has,' Beer Gut replied. 'Langdon said he owed it to us, the workers, to let us know what was goin' on before he finally left the construction site.'

'I think he's just making trouble,' Barrel Chest replied. 'That man's got no loyalty to anyone apart from himself. He's bitter about Challener getting' rid of him. If he can screw up Challener's attempts to prevent the strike worsening, he will.'

'How do we know Challener's gonna pay us all our full wages anyway? I thought the bank stopped offering him new loans,' the bearded man asked.

'They have except this one's secured against the sale of a mine and the railroad leading to it, and apparently the sale's been agreed,' Beer Gut pointed out. 'Langdon told me.'

'If you can trust what he says,' the bearded man commented.

'But from what we know,' Barrel Chest said, attempting to clarify the situation, 'no one's gonna lose out. No one's gonna end up being paid less than what they normally would have done, are they? The bond idea was clearly stupid; a desperate measure on Challener's part.'

'It was. You can't trade those bonds directly for whiskey,' Beer Gut agreed.

'So, theoretically, who could lose out?' the bearded man asked.

'All those who sold their bonds at below face value,' Beer

Gut pointed out, ''cos they were unable to make their cash last!'

'I know loads of those,' Barrel Chest admitted. 'The more you think about it, there could be problems. Challener might say, an' I can see his point if he did, that the only way he can afford to make good the wage deficit is to buy back the bonds he gave each of us at the value they were when he gave them to us.'

'That would be face value,' the bearded man emphasized.

'An' if we can't produce the bonds then he can't buy them back, so we don't get paid. If we speculated on the bonds by buying and selling them that's down to us and not his problem,' Barrel Chest continued, feeling that he was getting his head around this particular scenario. The men fell silent.

'I understand what you are saying,' Beer Gut responded after giving the matter more thought. 'I hope that Challener doesn't sell any of us short, that's all.'

'What do you think would happen if he did?' asked the bearded man.

'There would be a riot,' Beer Gut replied.

CHAPTER 20

Carew Langdon took a while to calm down and free his mind from the vice-like grip that had been causing him to fixate on his hatred for Burrell Challener. The red mist having cleared, he could now see that his attempts to spread malicious, contradictory rumours among the railroad construction workers about how Challener might pay them their back wages was childish and probably futile. He had finished getting mad and was now in a frame of mind to get even.

His plan was a remarkably simple one and made even more attractive from the perspective that the gang had already undertaken what turned out to be a dry run a few months ago, which bizarrely resulted in their employment by Burrell Challener. Langdon revelled in its simplicity; to rob Challener's wages train, that is to say, his personal railcar pulled by a small steam engine as it made its way slowly uphill through a wooded area on its way to the 'hell on wheels' town. Unlike last time, when the gang's efforts were prevented by Challener's men who were hiding out in the woods waiting to ambush the robbers, this time they would not be there.

Following the information given to him by the inhabitants of the tent town, Bose began his search for Griffen in the area

140

where it had been suggested that he was carrying out a track inspection. Bose rode for a few miles, systematically following the track back towards its origination point. He stopped his horse at the brow of a hill as the railroad rolled down a gradient and into a wooded area below.

'Wonder if Griffen's working down there in those woods,' he said to himself. His tracker's instinct told him that there might be trouble afoot. Bose decided to ride parallel to the railroad but high up, close to the top of the tree line, where it would be easier to make a getaway if needs be. He rode on for another half mile, until the area below him became covered in thick forest, before stopping again. Turning his horse to face the bottom of the valley below, he was able to catch glimpses of the rails through the trees. He felt the heat of the late afternoon sun on his back. Dismounting, he sat down on the slope of the forest floor and took out his small brass telescope.

'Well, I be damned,' he muttered to himself. 'Looks like someone's planning a hold-up!' Tying his horse to a tree, he took his Winchester rifle and walked quietly along the slope in search of a better viewing point. Finally, he found one, at the top of a path that had been cleared down the slope, presumably to transport supplies to the valley floor below. He concealed himself behind a rock at the top of the path and took another look. Adjusting the focus of his telescope, he could see that a large pile of wood had been laid over the track. Experience told him that this would be torched sooner or later to stop a train from going any further. That train, he realized, had to be Burrell Challener's wages train. He remembered the bearded man at the bar saying that its arrival was imminent.

Bose wondered if this could be another of Challener's scams so as not to have to pay his workers: to rob his own train. However, if that money didn't reach the workers, Bose knew that they wouldn't all be as rational as the man with the barrel chest and, as his companion with the beer gut had suggested, there could be a riot. A riot that could easily spread to Probity and make it a battleground for the 'have nots' to unleash their frustration on the 'haves'. He knew at all costs that he had to prevent that from happening. He didn't have to wait long for the opportunity.

'Here it comes men!' Carew Langdon exclaimed. 'Let's go.' The gang rode out of the forest and lit the bonfire of dry wood that they had piled across the tracks. They watched and waited until the bonfire was fully alight and then retired to the shelter of the trees.

'Do we put our masks on, boss?' one of Carew's trio of subordinates asked.

'No need. We want Challener to recognize us. We want him to see that it's us that's givin' 'im trouble.'

'But won't he shop us, boss?' one of the other gang members asked.

'No chance,' Carew replied confidently, 'because when that train arrives at that tent town up there with no money on board, Burrell Challener is gonna be facin' a lynch mob! An' he'll know that 'cos I'm gonna tell him. Yer see, I'm gonna ride most of the way up there with 'im. Make sure he gets there, tied to the fixtures and fittings of his railcar. Then, I'm gonna jump ship an' meet you boys over the state line as we agreed.'

'Yer don't think they'll believe him when he says it was us that robbed the train?' the third gang member asked.

'No. Not for one moment,' Carew Langdon said. 'The workers all feel sorry about what Challener's done to us. They think that we're one of them. They'll all think that Challener's tryin' to scam them.'

*

There was a screeching, grinding noise of metal against metal as the driver brought the locomotive to a halt in front of the bonfire that blocked its path. Challener's new security guard jumped down from the foot plate, gun in hand and ready for action, before falling dead on the ground from a bullet to the chest that had been fired at him from inside the forest. Four gunmen emerged from that spot.

'Mr Challener!' Carew Langdon exclaimed. 'Fancy meeting you here!'

'Nothin' fancy about meeting the likes of you, Langdon, I can assure you,' Burrell Challener replied. 'What do you want?'

'What do I want? It looks like you need some new security!' Carew Langdon jibed.

'I ain't lookin' to rehire you, if that's what yer thinking?'

'You ain't paid me or the boys yet for the last work we did for you,' Langdon pointed out. That's what we're here for. To collect. Understand you got a lot of money on board. Unpaid wages. Ain't that right, Challener? If you hand it all over, we'll let you be on your way!'

The first of Bose Hendry's rifle bullets hit one of Langdon's gang in the head. The second hit the second gang member in the arm, causing him to drop his weapon, while the third bullet hit him in the leg, forcing him to retire wounded into the forest.

'He's up there, behind the rock!' Carew Langdon shouted at his last gang member.

'I know, but I can't see him!' the two-bit outlaw shouted back. 'I'm lookin' straight into the sun. He's got the advantage! Aaah!' the outlaw screamed as Bose Hendry's fourth bullet secured that advantage and entered its victim's heart.

'Open the safe, Challener!' Langdon demanded, starting to panic.

'There ain't one,' Challener pointed out.

'What?'

'It ain't been fitted yet. The money is bagged up and inside the laundry basket under my desk here!' Carew Langdon couldn't believe his luck. A laundry basket – no safe to blow! This was going to be easier than taking candy from a baby! He lowered his gun and in total disbelief walked towards the train steps ready to get rich. His open posture made it easy for Bose Hendry's fifth bullet to fatally wound its intended victim.

Even though he was unaware of who his good Samaritan actually was, Burrell Challener knew it was a signal telling him to ride his luck. As the bonfire subsided, he shouted at the engine driver to release the locomotive's brakes and continue their journey.

'Well,' Bose Hendry muttered under his breath, as he got up from behind the rock. 'I've just saved your life, Burrell Challener. Now it's up to you to save your own.'

CHAPTER 21

'Have you got my money, Mr Challener?'

'Where's our wages, Challener?'

'You'd better have our money Challener!' The workers shouted out at the tops of their voices. The driver had stopped the locomotive on the track in the middle of the tent city. Scores of men thronged around it, preventing the train from reaching the siding that was its normal resting place. Burrell Challener emerged from his personal railcar and stood on the rear footplate with a megaphone in his hand. He raised the instrument to his mouth.

'Gentlemen!' he said. 'I have come here today to pay you your outstanding wages, not in bonds but in cash!' There was a large cheer and the men thronged around the railcar. 'I have great faith in you and this project, which is why I have sold some of the railroad's assets in order to be able to pay you your money and continue our investment, not mine note, nor yours, but our investment in this new railroad!' Another cheer went up. 'Now to keep this transaction simple, here's how I'm gonna pay you! Last pay day, because of problems with the bank that I have now resolved, I had to give you your wages partially in cash and partially in company bonds at face value! So today I'm gonna buy those bonds back from you at face value in cash. In other words, you give me back the bonds I gave you and in return I will give you the same value in cash. Is that clear?'

'I've already sold my bonds!' a voice in the crowd shouted out.

'Me too!' shouted another.

'Well that means you've already been paid for them, don't it. In other words,' Challener shouted through his megaphone, 'you an' I are square!'

'But I sold mine at less than their face value!' someone else shouted out. 'So I'm out of pocket! How you gonna make good the shortfall in my wages?'

'I ain't!' Burrell Challener pointed out. 'You shouldn't have sold them at too cheap a price!'

'I had to!' the man continued. 'I've got a family to feed. 'They can't eat bonds. I needed cash urgently to buy food!' Challener felt he needed to close this conversation down quickly. He felt an undercurrent of unrest starting to arise.

'Well,' he said with as much compassion as he could muster, 'go find the man you sold your bonds to and when I buy them back from him, ask him for the profit he made on the sale of yours.'

'But what if the man who bought my colleague's bonds on the cheap,' somebody else shouted out, 'has already sold them onto another worker? It starts to get messy to sort out, don't it, Challener?' Calling the railroad mogul by his surname should have been the warning sign for Burrell to back down or beat a hasty retreat but he chose to ignore it.

'Listen!' he spat the word out angrily through the megaphone. 'If this is gonna work at all, we need to keep it simple! If there are too many exceptions and complications, we will struggle to get to the bottom of who sold what to who and at what price! That's why I will buy bonds at face value in cash only if I am presented with them. Otherwise there is no deal. If you wanna go and find who you sold your bonds to and claim back any shortfall of cash you think you are owed from them that's fine, but if you haven't got any proof of sale I think you'll find it difficult to get your money back! If you sold your bonds on, that ain't my responsibility to sort out – it's yours but don't sort it out in company time!'

Burrell Challener may have got away with the bulk of that speech but the last sentence about responsibility was perhaps too honest for many of the men to stomach. A couple of shots were fired in the air but it was a small rock through the window of Burrell's new railcar that became the final invitation to retreat and goaded him into action. Walking back into the car, he locked the rear door behind him, and hurried through the carriage to the front footplate.

Raising the megaphone to his mouth, he shouted to the engine driver, 'Reverse, pronto!' As the locomotive's wheels slowly started to reverse and Challener secured the front door, locking himself in the railcar, an enraged worker jumped onto the footplate and smashed the butt of his rifle through the window in the carriage door. Instinctively, Burrell Challener spun round, unholstered his revolver and shot the would-be intruder through the chest. Others managed to climb onto the roof of the carriage but a few carefully placed bullets from Challener's Peacemaker soon removed them from that particular perch and warned off those co-workers who might have been considering a similar approach.

As the train began to pick up speed and pull away from the tent town, it was pursued by groups of riders on horseback, many armed with rifles but without the horsemanship to fire them at a moving target while at full gallop. However, the easier it became for Burrell Challener to start picking off some of the outliers, the more seemed to join the hunt.

'Drive faster!' he screamed at the engine driver through his megaphone. He needed to put sufficient distance between the train and the horsemen so that they would give up the chase.

'We can't go any faster!' the engine driver shouted back.

'This loco can go faster than this!' Burrell challenged the driver.

'It can but not just here!' the fireman explained.

'Who says?'

'Isham Griffen!' the driver replied. 'If we approach the brow of this hill too quickly, we will go into the descent on the other side too fast and risk derailing on the bend!'

'Rubbish!' Challener shouted back. 'Griffen always errs on the side of caution. Keep the speed up!'

The train desperately tried to cling to the rails but it was the tight curvature of the bend and the fact that it had picked up too much speed as it descended from the brow of the hill that caused it to leave the track. As they landed, the front bogies dug into the rocky ground, upending the locomotive and causing it to somersault, tender over engine. The railcar was tossed into the air, like a fish fighting for survival on the end of a fisherman's line, before being smashed against the rocks and leaving its shattered shell hanging over the cliff face.

The first group of riders from the tent city, who had witnessed the spectacle from afar, soon caught up with the derailed train and discovered the dead bodies of the fireman, the engine driver and Burrell Challener. All three had been flung from the wreckage. The concerns of the next group of riders to reach the scene had a different focus, however. They witnessed a laundry basket being flung from the damaged railcar and into the air before rolling down the slope towards the cliff edge.

All the riders watched aghast as the wicker basket rolled over the edge and bounced off the rocks below, while its contents – sacks of dollar bills – split open, leaving the money inside to fall gently, like confetti, into the Ravine River below.

CHAPTER 22

It had turned dark as Bose Hendry made his way back across the escarpment towards Probity, having failed to find any sign of Isham Griffen. Ironically, the darkness facilitated Hendry's search in a way that daylight never could. Indeed, Hendry had passed near to the spot where Griffen had pitched his tent much earlier on in the day without even realizing it was there. But the black of the night had made Griffen's assistant's lantern stand out like a beacon on the edge of the forest as its light flickered through the leaves on the trees. Approaching cautiously, Bose could make out the glowing embers of a small camp fire.

'Who goes there?' A voice boomed out of the darkness. Its owner slowly became visible, a young man carrying a buffalo rifle appeared out of the shadows.

'My name's Hendry,' Bose replied. 'I was after Mr Griffen. There's been a rumour of an accident, according to people I passed on the trail. Apparently, Burrell Challener's railcar has derailed on the other side of the tent city. They're sayin' it took a bend too fast. Maybe you'd already heard about it. If not, I thought Mr Griffen may want to be made aware and if needs be carry out an investigation.'

'Thanks, mister,' the young man said. 'No, I hadn't heard about it. Mr Griffen may have been aware but he's not here

149

at the moment.'

'Oh?' Bose grunted.

'No. Afraid not. He's gone to Probity. He said he had some urgent business to attend to there. Something to do with Hilliard Rainecourt, but I don't know what that might be.'

'Oh, I see,' said Bose, thoughtfully.

'Do you want some coffee, mister?' the young man asked, welcoming the chance of some company.

'No, I'd better be getting back to Probity,' Bose replied. 'But thanks for the offer.'

Eleanor's mother had made a quick recovery and she was therefore able to cut short her stay. She had sent a telegram to her mistress, Isabella, explaining the change in her itinerary and advising that she hoped to arrive back at the Rainecourts' residence before dark. Unfortunately, however, on the initial leg of her return journey the stagecoach in which she had planned to travel lost a wheel, so she had to wait for the next one. Still, she was now almost home and had managed to catch the last stage from the quayside up the cliff to Probity. Her walk across the square from the point of alighting was a brief albeit it lonely one given that most people were now in bed.

There were two entrances to the Rainecourt mansion, the grand front entrance with the imposing double doors and the trademan's entrance, at the side towards the back of the building. She chose to enter the property by the latter route, so as to avoid waking her mistress, whom she assumed would be alone in bed. It was the first day of the month, when Mr Rainecourt regularly hosted a private dinner for the heads of the local chambers of commerce, an all-male preserve, on board the *Pride of Probity* and he invariably would end up spending the night there.

As she entered the dark alleyway at the side of the house, she instinctively looked behind her to check that she wasn't being followed. There was no one there, however, and she felt reassured that on this occasion her instincts could be ignored and put their arousal down to her mind playing tricks. Having denied her body's early warning system of potential danger, she was totally unprepared for the piece of rock that was brought down hard on her head and cracked her skull. At the point of contact she fell unconscious to the ground. She did not feel her pulse being checked for any signs of life, nor was she aware of being dragged into the undergrowth because by then she was already dead.

Isabella Rainecourt stirred in her sleep and turned over. She wasn't sure whether it was the moonlight shining across her through the gap in the curtains or a dull tapping noise from outside that was preventing her from continuing her slumbers but suddenly she was wide awake. She wondered if she had been woken by the noise of Eleanor coming home.

'Mrs Rainecourt, Mrs Rainecourt,' a man's voice whispered. 'Are you awake?' A cold shiver went down Isabella's spine. The dull tapping noise occurred again. It was someone on the other side of the bedroom door, which she had dutifully locked.

'Who . . . who is it she stammered nervously?'

'It is I, Isham Griffen.' Isabella felt a lump rise in her throat as he tried the bedroom door handle. 'I see you have locked your room door. Very sensible. You must keep it locked until I come back for you. I have some important business to attend to. It shouldn't take long.'

'What is going on, Isham? I don't understand, please tell me!'

'When I come back, I will tell you all. But as I expected,

nowhere is safe. There are rumours everywhere that the rail-road workers are mutinying. It means big trouble. Nowhere is safe.'

'Are matters really that serious?' Isabella asked. 'You make it sound like, like Armageddon. A matter of life and death.'

'I'm afraid it is. People are saying that Burrell Challener is dead, killed in a rail accident. But it is worse than that. It is much closer to home than that.'

'How do you mean?' Isabella asked nervously. Isham Griffen paused.

'OK. I will tell you briefly but then I must go. Your maid Eleanor is dead. I found her slumped under a bush in the alleyway at the side of the house. At first I thought she may have been drinking but on closer inspection it was obvious that she was dragged there after being hit on the head by a rock.' Isabella sank down on the bed overcome with shock. She leant over to Hilliard's beside cabinet, removed his hip flask and took a sip of whiskey.

'Mrs Rainecourt, are you still there? Are you all right?' Isham Griffen demanded to know.

'Yes,' said Isabella regaining her composure. 'It's just . . . it's just two deaths, Seth Challener and now my dear Eleanor, and you are always the one on hand with an explanation.'

'Are you accusing me of murdering your damned maid?' Isham Griffen asked angrily.

'No, of course not. It's the shock of the untimely death of someone close to me and the coincidence; I barely know you and it is the second suspicious death in a very short space of time that you are admitting you have become caught up in.'

'I thought you trusted me, Mrs Rainecourt. Now you have given me grounds for doubt,' Isham Griffen said coldly.

'Oh, I do trust you, Mr Griffen! I do!' Isabella pleaded.

'Well, when I come back for you, you will have to prove it to me. Otherwise, our relationship won't work. I must go now but I will be back before the dawn breaks.' There was a brief noise on the other side of the door and then silence. Isabella took another sip of whiskey to fortify herself and walked over to the bedroom door. She slowly but quietly unlocked the door to let herself out and pulled down on the door handle but it wouldn't move. She tried again with more force but still the handle refused to budge. He's wedged a chair under it, she thought to herself. He's locked me in!

Hilliard had always warned her to keep a gun close by at all times. She looked in his bedside cabinet but to no avail. Clearly, he had heeded his own advice and no doubt had both his Peacemaker and his Derringer with him right now. Isabella had tried to convince her husband that it was unnecessary to always carry a firearm but given her current predicament she began to understand why she may have failed.

Desperate, she rummaged around in her own bedroom cabinet and her spirits lifted as her fingers found her own pocket Derringer. She took out the gun, released the safety catch and swivelled the twin barrels upwards on their shared hinge, only to reveal that the gun wasn't loaded. The ammunition was locked away in Hilliard's gun cupboard downstairs, where for safe keeping she always maintained it should be.

CHAPTER 23

As he returned from the range, Bose Hendry found the out-skirts of Probity a hive of activity. Sheriff McKendrick was manning a road block with a hastily assembled posse of deputies.

'Hendry,' the sheriff said by way of a greeting. 'Anythin' goin' on out there? Can we expect raging railroad workers makin' their way here to get their hands on their money?'

'It's quiet out there at the moment,' Bose replied. 'I'd heard that Challener's wages train got derailed and the money ended up in the river.'

'That's right,' the sheriff said. 'We've got a small, heavily armed flotilla blocking the river a little way upstream from the quayside. So far, it's been quiet down there as well. They've been fishin' dollar bills out of the river by the score. It's strange, I thought we'd have hordes down there, jumpin' into the river tryin' to fish out the money for themselves and those who were unsuccessful smashin' the place up!'

'That latter thought certainly did pass through my mind, Sheriff, if I hadn't have stopped the Langdon Gang from robbing that wages train,' Bose admitted. 'It's right to err on the side of caution but maybe we've underestimated them. Maybe there are more rational, sensible-minded men amongst their number than we've given them credit for.'

'How d'yer mean, Hendry?'

'Well, their fight – the one they can win – is not with Probity, it's with the remaining directors of Challener's railroad company. That company still has saleable assets and the workers will know that a lot of that cash that ended up in the river will never be recovered, with some of it at least having been swallowed by the fish!'

'It'll break the company if the workers hijack its assets and demand they are sold,' Sheriff McKendrick said.

'And then we can all sleep comfortably in our beds!' Bose Hendry pointed out. 'So, you haven't stopped anyone down by the river but what about up here?'

'Only one person. Isham Griffen. Said he had some business to deal with in town. He's the least likely person to cause trouble, so we let him through.'

The quayside was quiet when Bose got down there as if the whole town had gone into lockdown. He tied his horse to the rail outside one of the bars and walked towards the *Pride of Probity*.

'Run, Mr Hendry, run!' the purser shouted at him. Bose realised they were loosening the mooring ropes of the paddle steamer and had withdrawn the landing stages. Starting at the back of the quay, he took a running jump and just managed to clear the widening gap of water between the paddle steamer and the quay.

'What's goin' on?' Bose asked the purser, as the boat moved away from the quay.

'Just a precaution in case the railroad workers come here to threaten us. We'll drop anchor in the middle of the river. We're less vulnerable to any unwanted boarders there.'

'I don't think they're comin',' Bose said. 'Rioters are fuelled by anger and act on impulse. They would have been here by now. Any anger towards Probity, however misguided, will have long subsided. They're up to something else.'

'Are you after Mr Rainecourt?' Bose nodded. 'He's in the smoking room.'

'Damn,' Isham Griffen said quietly to himself, as he overheard the purser talking to Hendry and watched the boat drift away from the quayside. He had walked down the zigzag, keeping close to the shadows, and had narrowly escaped being seen by Hendry, who had ridden down on horseback. He walked along the quayside and at the far end found a small skiff complete with oars, moored to the side. Upstream, he could just make out the lights of the flotilla, which was too far away to see or bother him. He undid the mooring rope and boarded the skiff. With the aid of the oars and the current, he allowed the skiff to drift along the far side of the paddle steamer. As the skiff reached the *Pride of Probity*'s bow, Griffen tied the small boat to it and hauled himself on board.

'I haven't seen Griffen,' Hilliard admitted. 'It's one of the few nights that I know everybody on board!'

'When did you last visit your room?' Bose asked.

'Oh, it was a few hours ago. Everything was OK. As I left, I made sure that all the windows and the door were locked. Anyway, thanks for the warning and good night. Get the purser to give you a cabin.' Bose watched him walk off into the distance and then stop to light a cigar and have a chat with one of his guests.

As Hilliard walked away, Bose looked over the side of the paddle steamer and noticed the skiff tied to the bow. On one hand, he realized that it could have been perfectly innocent, but on the other? He ran up two flights of stairs to the hurricane deck and looked over the side rail. The windows of Hilliard Rainecourt's personal suite were open, leaving the curtains flapping in the breeze. Surely, Rainecourt couldn't have made it back already? There was no sign of light coming from the room. Bose needed to find Rainecourt before he reached his suite. Griffen may have already broken in and could be sitting there in the dark awaiting Rainecourt's return, having opened the windows to release the stifling heat that would have built up throughout the day. An engineer of his standing would have no problem in picking an internal door lock. Bose ran back to the centre of the boat to try and find Hilliard.

'Good evening, Mr Rainecourt. Lock the door behind you and throw me the key!' Seeing that Isham Griffen was armed with a revolver, Hilliard did as he was asked.

'Griffen! What do you want?'

'I've come to settle old scores. You have destroyed my dream engineering project of bringing the railroad to Probity and you have deceived the woman I have fallen in love with.'

'What woman are you talking about? Tilly? I knew this would come out sooner or later. Look, there was nothing going on of an amorous nature between me and Tilly. It was a business arrangement. My wife and I couldn't have children and I wondered if it was me. Provided I paid her a considerable fortune, Tilly offered to bear me a child. She had had one from a previous relationship and I have been desperate to sire a male heir for a long time. As it turned out, the problem is me, so I have paid her off. She is all yours.'

'I am not talking about Tilly. I am talking about your wife, Isabella. That is the woman I am in love with and I think she soon will be with me, especially when I tell her what you have just told me. She has had her suspicions about you. With you out of the way, Isabella will be mine along with your fortune. I am very focused when I am determined. That's why I killed your maid earlier on, as I did Seth Challener. You see, neither do I like people who cheat on me, nor those who can get in the way of me achieving my ambitions.'

'Isabella will never believe you!' Hilliard Rainecourt said. He was in a state of shock as he began to realize that he was dealing with a madman who was suffering from delusions and fixations.

'She will, because she will rationalize that avoiding the public disgrace brought about by your extramarital activity must have been the reason for your suicide!'

'What suicide?' Hilliard asked, feeling scared.

'This one,' Isham replied coldly. 'Here,' he stuffed a pillow over Hilliard's face as he collapsed on the floor. 'Now, I am going to give you this gun. It's very powerful because I've customized it. Don't try anything funny 'cos I'll blast your head off with this one.' He unholstered a second revolver. 'Now point the barrel through the pillow at your mouth. We don't want to wake anyone up, do we? Now, on the count of five I want you to pull the trigger. If you haven't by the time I count to six, I'll shoot you through the head. Ready? One . . . two . . . three . . . four . . .'

A single shot shattered the silence of the darkened room, with the bullet felling Isham Griffen as it entered his forehead. Bose Hendry climbed in through the window.

'You OK?' he asked.

'Yes,' Hilliard replied in a weak voice. 'Thanks to you. Did you hear everything?'

'Yes, afraid so.'

'Will you tell Isabella?'

'No, I think you should do that.'

'Do you think she will ever forgive me?'

'Eventually, yes.'

EPILOGUE

It was a few months after the demise of Isham Griffen and the railroad he had designed that Bose Hendry had occasion to ride through Probity again. On the surface he perceived that little had changed but deeper down, in many ways, he thought there had been a transformation.

Rails still ran across the escarpment but they were rusting and track laying had ceased months ago. There were barely any visible signs that a 'hell on wheels' tent town had ever existed. That was all largely to do with the fact that Hilliard Rainecourt had bought the land from the Ravine River Railroad Company. He'd paid little more than a song for it and was content to let it remain idle, for the time being at least.

Sitting at a quayside bar and reading the local paper, Bose discovered what had happened to the construction workers. Three of them had persuaded the rest that attacking Probity would have been an act of wanton destruction and would have resulted in them being branded as violent outlaws, rather than rebels with a just cause. He recognized the three of them from their photographs: the man with the beard, the one with the barrel chest and the other one with the beer gut. They had persuaded their fellow workers that the more constructive path would be to hijack some of the company's rolling stock and only release it if they were paid not only their cash wages in full but also given a redundancy payment. Realizing that an asset embargo and subsequent sale would have sent the company into liquidation, and in order to salvage their own reputations, the company directors financed the workers' demands from their extensive personal fortunes.

The task of deciding what to do with the land his father had obtained from the railroad would eventually be left to Hilliard Rainecourt's legally adopted son and heir. The child's adoptive mother, Isabella, explained to a delighted Bose that she and her husband had set up a new charity for orphaned children with the money that the townsfolk had fished from the river as a result of Burrell Challener's train derailment. Both Isabella and Hilliard had thought that the adoption of an orphaned boy would be the perfect solution for repairing their marital differences and as a result she was pleased to admit that the bond between them had never been stronger.